THE
HEiGHTS

BRIAN JAMES

SQUARE
FISH

FEiWEL AND FRiENDS
New York, NY

To Emily B. — for creating such
timeless characters.

SQUARE
FISH

An Imprint of Macmillan

THE HEIGHTS. Copyright © 2009 by Brian James. All rights reserved.
Distributed in Canada by H.B. Fenn and Company Ltd.
Printed in November 2009 in the United States of America by R. R. Donnelley
& Sons Company, Harrisonburg, Virginia. For information, address
Square Fish, 175 Fifth Avenue, New York, NY 10010.

Square Fish and the Square Fish logo are trademarks of Macmillan and are
used by Feiwel and Friends under license from Macmillan.

Library of Congress Cataloging-in-Publication Data Available

ISBN: 978-0-312-60736-4

Originally published in the United States by Feiwel and Friends
Square Fish logo designed by Filomena Tuosto
First Square Fish Edition: 2010

10 9 8 7 6 5 4 3 2 1

www.squarefishbooks.com

ONE

Always near the bay, I've felt like a fish. Pushed along through every day of my life the way fish are by the currents. Not caring much where the streams take me..never struggling this way or that. I'm fine with just drifting forward..moving in and out of the sunbeams like the cars move in and out of the fog on the city's highways. Never sure where I'm going..just that I'm going somewhere different than where I am.

Catherine says I feel that way because I was born in March..because I'm a water sign.

I asked her once what that had to do with anything.

—It has everything to do with everything, Henry— she told me. —It's the reason you're the way you are. Everything is written in the stars— saying it like it was the easiest thing in the world to understand because that's the way Catherine is.. any question can be figured out by whatever idea pops into her head first.

The way I think of things is never as direct as hers.. more like the rise and fall of the tide before the water breaks against the rocks. Always like the waves brought by a storm.. like how there's too much water and not enough space. My feelings fight inside me like that. Push up against each other.. pushing one out of the way to let another take over.

I feel it happening now as I watch Catherine walking out of our school. My nervousness giving way to something better when I see the wind pick up off the bay like it's attracted to her. The sun clears away the clouds, lifts the shadows, and gives a warm color to her skin. I haven't been waiting more than five minutes, but it still feels like I've been waiting my whole life. Every day feels like that.. like I only exist for her.

She tucks her hair away from the breeze and waves to me all in one slight and simple motion that blends so easily with her smile.. her eyes pulling me toward her like a magnet as I push myself away from the tree I'm leaning against. It's only once I start toward her that I see she's not alone. There's a group of her friends trailing behind her.. after her.. crowding her like a net strangling a butterfly.

I'm not sure *friends* is the right word to call them.. more like parasites. Except Nelly, not one of them care about her.. or about one another. They just care about making her just like them.. a survival instinct to increase their number of clones. They don't see that she's special in any way. They don't even want her to be special. They want her to be the same..want everyone to be the same. I can't stand when she's around them..the way they make her feel like shit for being different..for being better.

She never sees it like that.

She needs me to see it for her..to keep her safe from their popularity traps..from the people who just want to strip away all the beautifully strange parts that make her the most perfect girl in the world.

I feel the shift inside me again..the waves swaying as my feet stomp the ground with an angry pace. I clench my hands until my fingers turn white..my eyes screaming as I walk up to her but keeping the rest of me calm because she hates when I'm mean. I have to do my best to hide it..to play nice..play along just until I can get her away.

It's not so hard. Around her I can usually stay calm just by glancing over at her every few seconds. Catherine's always been able to settle me down like that.

—Hey, you ready?— I ask..cutting into the middle of the conversation and getting a series of nasty looks in return from everyone except her. But even Catherine's smile softens..disappears almost completely when she turns to the other girls and tells them she'll see them tomorrow.

—C'mon— I say..taking her hand in mine.

I feel better once we're walking away..once we're alone. I always do. I don't know why being alone with her makes such a difference..why I can't be myself unless it's just us. Maybe it would be different if I'd been born in the winter like her. Maybe if I were a Capricorn like Catherine, I wouldn't get so crazy about things the way I sometimes do.

Everything would be —*perfectly reasonable*— just how she always says it is.

But then again, if I wasn't the way I am.. and if she wasn't the way she is.. maybe we wouldn't be so perfect for each other.

—*It's the reason we get along so well*— Catherine's always telling me. She says our astrological signs are compatible.. that the earth needs the water just like we need each other.

I love the sound of her voice when she says —*We need each other*— I hear it in my head as we walk away the last of the afternoon.. playing it back over and over as the clouds linger above the path leading us through Fort Point Park.. her fingers between mine and even though we don't say a thing, I can still hear the words she's told me nearly every day since the day we met. —*We need each other*—

I don't remember much about that day, but I remember the cold. It found its way into the center of my bones like a ghost passing through my skin. I remember being alone.. wandering the city by myself until her father found me —*Where's your mother, son?*— he asked but I was too frozen to answer. I didn't know the answer. I'm not sure there was an answer because I'm not sure that I wasn't born on that day.. born five years old and shivering.

I can remember him gathering me in his arms and carrying me to his car. I remember the headlights cutting through the night like the glowing eyes of an overgrown insect. Then he brought me to his house and I saw her standing at the top of the stairs. I remember her perfectly. I remember her hair was like a sunset drawn with red crayons. And when she smiled at me, her face was warm. It was the first time the cold ever left me.

Catherine was different than anyone else in the world. I knew it just by staring at her. She wasn't just another girl..more like a star plucked from the sky and trapped between tiny bones..a star capturing heat that I could hold on to for warmth. My very own star that I knew would guide me forever as long as I held on tight and never let go. It's the only thing I've ever understood as easily as she seems to understand everything.

—Henry? What are you thinking about? I mean right now, what are you thinking about?— she asks me suddenly. Her voice always has a way of pulling me back from my thoughts..pulling me toward her no matter how far away I've drifted.

I hold her hand a little tighter as we walk.

—You know..just about things— I say.

She smiles softly like the dawn. —I think I do— she says.

The air fills with the sudden sound of cars driving on the Golden Gate Bridge, suspended high above as we pass under. Once we're on the other side, we'll start to climb up the hill that will bring us just as high..alongside Baker Beach and all the way down to Sea Cliff Avenue where our home sits a few yards from the steep rocks that look down into the ocean. Until then, we're alone. The entire city of San Francisco fades away behind us. The school day disappears into the past. Nothing exists except Catherine and me walking together like we've done every day that I can remember.

She glances over at the wind whipping across the brown

surface of the water in the distance. A flock of gulls take off like balloons set free from a child's hand, floating forever up to heaven when the gust hits. Catherine watches them like they're something made of magic.

Her hair gets swept across her face and I watch her hands tuck the longer strands behind her ears. It slides through her palm the same as it did the night we met . . still the same motion of her wrist at sixteen as she had when we were five.

—Do you ever wonder what it would be like to be with them?— she asks.

—Be like with who?— I ask. Her eyes wander up to the sky, borrowing the color from it. I know then that she means the birds. —The seagulls?— I say . . thinking as I talk . . imagining myself in flight. —I don't think it would be much different from this— I tell her. —I mean, it would be different just because we were flying . . but I doubt it would feel any different—

I can see her tongue pushing against the inside of her cheek the way it always does when she's thinking. She considers my opinion for as long as it takes to climb up the last steep hill before the path flattens again, giving us a perfect glimpse of the taller buildings that peek in and out between the trees . . the downtown buildings that always draw your eyes to the pyramid rising higher than the rest. Catherine stares at it for a moment before spinning around to face me again. —But how could it not feel different?— she asks. Her words sound small and curious. Then she pulls her hand away from mine and stops walking as if standing still will help her understand. She places her hands on her hips . . leans her weight on one leg and demands that I either agree with her or give a better answer.

I struggle for words.. trying to let my thoughts settle into little pools that are easier to collect than waves. It's easier to think when she's around.. easier to steady the storm. —*Well*— I say —I mean.. it's like if you were a bird.. and I was a bird.. we'd still be you and me just with wings and feathers and stuff like that. But we'd still be us.. we'd still be talking about this, just the other way around—

Catherine narrows her eyes. She studies me and I can almost see her trying to work out what I've said. —Okay, I guess that sort of makes sense— she says. She takes my hand again and starts walking again. —But I still think it would be different— she tells me. —I think I'd feel dizzy always going up so high and swooping back down—

She starts laughing and I can't help but smile. We've always been contagious to each other in that way. I've never doubted that it's why Mr. Earnshaw let me stay.. let me grow up as one of the family and gave me his last name even though Earnshaw means wealthy and Caucasian and I was just a scrawny orphan with Mexican skin. He did it because I've always been able to make Catherine smile and he's just as addicted to her smile as I am.

The sun breaks in and out of the leaves as we walk.. the shadows of so many trees dancing under our feet. I steal glances at Catherine but she's gone somewhere else.. staring off into the horizon like she's trying to memorize the different shades of copper blue that streak the sky. She only comes back because I squeeze her hand tighter.. bringing her closer to me .. a reflex that happens whenever the breeze catches the faint scent of soap from her skin.

Her body goes soft like she's just waking up .. her chin resting on her shoulder when she looks at me .. facing the sun so that her freckles fade in the glare, asking me if she's drifted off again.

I nod. —Don't worry about it—

Catherine takes a deep breath .. stretching out her arms as she comes alive. —You know what Mrs. Crane said today?— she asks. I shake my head. Mrs. Crane is our homeroom teacher and Catherine's physics teacher and is capable of saying just about anything .. most of it guaranteed to be insane. —She said I daydream too much— Catherine tells me.

—That's because she's crazy— I say and we both laugh .. but mine is fake .. half fake anyway because what I'm really thinking is how I'd like to run back there and tell Mrs. Crane what a lousy bitch I think she is.

—Yeah, I guess— Catherine says but she lowers her head .. keeps her eyes on the ground as her shoes step over stray leaves. —You don't think she's right, do you?— she asks, suddenly looking at me.

—Are you serious?— A hint of anger in my voice because I hate when she doubts herself .. when all the things other people say creep in and make her forget how much better than them she really is. It's why I have to protect her .. shield her from all the bullshit the world throws at us.

Her mouth forms the shape of a question when she bites her bottom lip .. she shrugs her shoulder and says —Maybe— She says sometimes she gets so completely lost in what she's thinking about that it's like she disappears. —Does that make me weird?—

—I don't think you should worry about anything Crazy Crane says— I tell her and she tells me that's not what she means.. not really anyway. —Then what are you talking about?— I ask.

—I don't know.. nothing I guess— she says. —It's just.. sometimes I think I should pay more attention to things.. try to be more like everyone else, you know?—

—No. I don't— I tell her honestly. —Being like everyone else is boring. Besides.. you're interesting and they all suck—

She smiles differently then.. a secret smile when she says —thanks— and begins swinging her arms.. playfully digging her elbow into my side.. letting me know I've said enough to stop her from worrying for now.

We see the house as soon as we reach the sidewalk. The steepled roof catches the light, making it look like a house out of a fairy tale. Not that every house in the Heights doesn't already look that way.. each with its own view of the cliffs where the sidewalks fall into the ocean.. with their endless mazes of rooms and expensive furniture.. but there's something about ours that seems better and makes all the others fade into the scenery. Maybe it's the soft white color that seems to hold on to the twilight even after the sun has set.. or maybe it's the large windows on the fourth floor that look into Catherine's room on one side and mine on the other. Or maybe it's just because it's home.

Whatever it is, I've always thought our house was really Heaven in disguise. Sometimes instead of thinking I was born the day Mr. Earnshaw found me, I think it's really the day I died. But either way it doesn't matter.. dead or alive doesn't matter.. as long as every day ends with me being washed up on its porch, I'll be fine. Because as long as there's the house, there will always be Catherine.

Nothing else will ever mean anything to me.

⚔

I want to kiss Henry.

I've never kissed him. Not the way I want to. I've only ever kissed him the way we did as little kids. A quick touch of our lips and that's it. But sometimes, I want to kiss him differently. I want to kiss him the way Nelly's always kissing boys. The way I've only ever pretended to kiss other boys, but never really meant it.

I think everything would immediately make sense if we kissed that way.

We'd know right away if we were meant to be brother and sister, or if we were meant to be soul mates. It would just happen instantly. Poof! The same kind of magic that turns frogs into princes. He either becomes my prince or he stays a frog and at least then I'd know.

There's always been this kind of confusion between us of how we're supposed to be with each other. It's been there from the beginning, since my dad first found him on the side of the road the same way Nelly's dad found a puppy once. But I could tell just by the way he looked at me that we'd be together for the rest of our lives. It's the kind of thing you know the same way birds know how to fly or fish know how to swim. What I don't know is just how exactly we're going to fit together. That's why I've made up my mind to kiss him tonight.

Part of me wants to tell him, but I figure it's probably better not to say anything. I don't want it to feel too planned. But I don't want him to be freaked out either. I mean, maybe I'm way off. Maybe he only thinks of me as a best friend. That would be a disaster.

He wraps his hand tighter around mine and I feel myself go weak.

"Did I drift off again?" I ask and he nods. He's used to it, though, and tells me not to worry about it. Daydreaming's a bad habit, though. I do it all the time. Sometimes I forget that other people aren't part of them. Like with the birds a few minutes ago. I imagined flying over the city and looking down on all the people scattered on every block, wandering in different directions, and wondered what it must look like to the seagulls. I forgot that Henry wasn't imagining it too and I just blurted out and asked him something that probably didn't make any sense.

I know he doesn't mind, but it bothers me sometimes. I worry about going off on these tangents. About people thinking I'm strange. I know my teachers do. They're always calling my name and snapping their fingers to bring me out of these trances. Today was the worst. My head was full of thoughts about princes and frogs and happily ever afters. My physics teacher lost it. She doesn't have any patience for that kind of behavior as it is, so she certainly couldn't handle the way I was acting today.

"You know what Mrs. Crane said today? She said I daydream too much," I tell Henry. He tells me that's because she's crazy and

I give a polite laugh, thinking about her Einstein hairdo and the way her eyes are always wiry like she's had too much caffeine. "Yeah, I guess," I agree. She is kind of crazy, but that doesn't mean she's wrong. "You don't think she's right, do you?" I ask.

"Are you serious?" he says.

There's something in his voice that makes me wish I never said anything. Something that lets me know he's going to say something to her tomorrow in homeroom. It's going to cause trouble, but I can't take it back now. Might as well go forward. So, I bite my bottom lip and shrug.

"Maybe," I mumble. Maybe I'm just being paranoid, but lately I've felt kind of out of place. It's sort of why I want to figure out about me and him. Because falling in love with him is either part of what makes me strange or part of what will make me not care so much. I can't explain any of that to him without giving away too much. So I stick to the other things that worry me. I tell him about how I've been so spacey lately. "It's like I disappear and don't even realize it. Does that make me weird?"

He says I shouldn't worry about anything Mrs. Crane says.

"That's not really what I mean," I say. I start to bite my nails when he asks me to explain it more. "I don't know," I say, shaking my head. "Nothing, I guess." I'm lying, I just don't know how to say what I'm trying to say. What I'm really trying to ask him is whether or not it's completely wrong to feel the way I do about him because I know it's not normal. So I find a different way to say it. I ask him if he thinks I should try to be more like everyone else.

"No. I don't. Being like everyone else is boring," he says. I want to tell him that it might be boring, but that it also makes things easier. But then he smiles at me and the words go away. I get lost in his eyes that are almost as black as his hair. Usually he's staring off into the distance, like he's watching something in the future that the rest of us can't see, but every once in a while he stares right at me. It freaks most of our friends out when Henry stares at them like that, but not me. Maybe because with me, there's always the smile too. His real smile, not the one he uses for taking pictures. It's a smile he only really gives to me. "Besides," he says. "You're interesting and they all suck."

I smile then because I know I'm special to him. I've always known it, but it's still nice when he says it. Makes me care less about being normal. It's his way of trying to protect me from myself.

He's always trying to protect me from everything. Even when we were little. He'd get so crazy if anyone tried to pick on me. I remember the first time he came to my rescue. His first day of school with me. There was this boy Philip who always pulled at my ponytail. Held on to it and teased me until my eyes would get pink and then he'd chant, "Crybaby Catherine," until the other kids laughed at me. Well, he tried it on Henry's first day and never tried it again.

Henry knocked him down the second Philip's fingers grabbed for me. It startled me. The way Henry went off so suddenly like an explosion. The way Philip fell like something that had been broken. I remember being afraid at first by how Henry was standing over him like he wanted to do something worse than just knock him on the ground. It was like he snapped or something.

But then he looked at me and it was like everything stopped.

He stopped.

And I knew then that he would always come back to me. That he'd always be gentle with me because I'd always be able to calm him. The stars made it that way, that we'd always be able to balance each other out. I've always thought it's a sign that we're meant to be together. I just hope Henry thinks so too. And if he doesn't think it already, maybe he will after we kiss.

I don't know what I'll do if he doesn't. I don't know who I am if Henry isn't nearby. It's like what the star sign books say about one sign getting strength from another. Like they feed each other. Henry's like that for me. Sort of like a brother and a boyfriend all in one. I could never live without him.

As soon as we turn onto our street, I see someone waiting on our porch. I know right away who it is, but I still ask if it's Hindley because it's such a surprise to see him. He hasn't been to visit in almost a year. Not since he got married and got a big promotion. He thinks he's all grown up now. I guess he assumes that means he shouldn't come home anymore even though he only lives in Los Angeles. It's only a short flight back here to San Francisco, but he acts like it's a world away. It makes him feel important. He's always been rotten like that, but he's still my brother. I'm still happy to see him.

It's more than I can say for Henry, that's for sure.

"What's he doing home?" he says, making it sound like Hindley is some kind of infection. I can't blame him, though. Hindley has always treated him horribly. I don't know why. It's not Henry's fault Dad always liked him a little better. Dad would like Hindley just as much if he didn't act so spoiled.

Hindley never saw it that way, though. He thought Henry was trying to steal our family from us. Then he'd go off about how all Mexicans are thieves. It made me so mad. I hate him when he talks like that.

I used to try to make them get along but they bring out the

worst in each other. So now I just try to keep them apart. If they want to act like jerks to each other, that's fine. I choose to love both of them anyway.

I break free and start running once Hindley spots me. I really can't wait to see him. I nearly knock him down when I leap into his arms and we both start laughing. He's strong enough to catch me, though. He sets me down easy. I have a million questions running through my head and try to get them out all at once. I want to know what he's been up to and how long he's staying. And I do really want to know, I'm not just asking to ask. It's funny because we never really got along too well when he lived here. We were always at each other's throats because I would take Henry's side in every battle between them. But now that we don't see each other and hardly talk, we're somehow closer. It's strange how that happens with some people. How being far apart brings you closer.

"Hey, Cathy, slow down!" he says. He doesn't bother to say anything to Henry. He barely even glances at him, moping up the steps.

"Does Dad know you're coming?" I ask. "If he does, he never mentioned it. I wish he did. I think everything's a mess inside. He really should have said something. Is he home? I want to tell him I'm mad at him." I start to head in, ready to search the front rooms for my father, who's probably watching us and laughing. Hindley stops me, though. He takes my arm and tells me to wait a minute.

His smile fades away then. His perfect posture slowly slouches and I can tell he's trying to look anywhere except at me. That's when I realize that something's happened. He's not just here to visit, I can tell. His expression is making me start to worry. Then he lowers his head and I know whatever it is he's going to tell me is something that means nothing will ever be the same again.

Henry notices it too but won't say anything.

My eyes dart back and forth, waiting for one of them to speak. But they both stay buttoned up and I'm forced to be the one to ask what's going on. "What happened?"

Hindley takes forever to say anything and I can feel my hands shaking because I know he's only stalling. "I didn't want them to tell you before you got home," he says. I bring my hands up to my mouth to keep every part of me from screaming at him to get it out. But I already know. The way he puts his hands on my shoulders tells me. It's the same way Dad told me about Mom dying the month before Henry came. "There was an accident this morning. They told me he couldn't have felt any pain."

I want to tell him that I feel pain, though.

I feel like I'm being slowly torn open, like a carefully wrapped present.

The only word I'm able to say is no. I say it so many times that it doesn't even sound like a word. It's a reflex. Like if I say it enough it'll reverse everything. I don't know why, but every thought I've had all day starts running through my mind while Hindley's trying to talk to me. He's telling me all the things he's supposed to. Saying everything will be okay and that we'll get through this, but I can't help thinking about birds flying over the bay. I feel so stupid for everything I've thought about today. My dad was somewhere dying. Worrying about me probably while I was wasting time worrying if people thought I was weird or not.

Henry moves closer to me when I start to cry. I don't see him as much as sense him. His shadow or maybe just the feel of him. I know it's safe to let go then. I know he'll catch me when I shatter, so I fall into his arms like the pieces of a broken rainbow.

TWO

———— ⁂ ————

I stay close to the back of the room . . hugging the wall and hiding behind all the mingling guests that fill the parlor. They buzz and circle one another like a swarm around a hive . . the clinking of glasses like the hum of wings . . the collected volume of their whispering like the hiss of a stinger before it digs in. I watch them and wish I could blend into the walls . . only the walls are white like their skin . . mine stands out like a shadow in a bright room.

—Who is that again? Oh, right, the orphan— a lady says . . close enough for me to hear but she doesn't seem to be bothered by being rude. She even has the nerve to give me a sympathetic smile after. She's not the first one to wonder who I am . . to stare at me in a way that makes me feel like an outsider in my own home . . at my father's own funeral. I bet most of them didn't even know my dad. They're only here because he was an important person in this town and being here shows others how important they are. They don't care about him . . or how his being gone will affect me or Catherine. They only care about feeling important.

All of them are so full of themselves it makes me sick.

All the men in their expensive suits wear frowns as they step through the door and shake Hindley's hand . . pass along a few sad words as he passes back a sorry look. The women all tell him to be strong . . moving their mouths slowly . . lipstick smiles to brighten up their dark clothing. Hindley and his wife, Frances, make little comments under their breath . . a quiet thank-you before the guests become part of the social event of the year.

Even from across the room, I can tell it's all an act.

I'm glad Hindley didn't ask me to take part in it. He thinks not asking bothers me. It's his way of showing he doesn't consider me a full member of the family. Whatever. It's not like it's anything new. He's never liked me. It's no secret. It's also no secret that I hate shit like this . . these gatherings . . they're games just like the ones the popular kids at school are always playing. If Hindley really wanted to get under my skin, he'd have asked me to greet the wealthy assholes as they walked through the door. He'd make me shake hands with all the powerful people in the city as they looked down on me.

Catherine and I call them the little lords.

They're the people who sit in the offices downtown that reach into the sky . . the kind of people who command the world around them like it's a toy. They pretend to be so refined but really they're no better than their spoiled kids who stomp their feet on the floor whenever they don't get their way. Mr. Earnshaw was never like that. He tolerated them because he had to, but he always warned us against growing up to be like that. He never wanted any of us to be someone who nods at everything everybody says without thinking. He didn't want us to be them. Too bad it didn't take with Hindley . . he acts just as privileged as the rest of them.

Mr. Earnshaw would get a kick out of this circus if he were here. He'd tell me —Buck up, Henry. Be polite and it'll all be over soon— I'd do it for him. I'd make petty conversations with our neighbors Edgar and Isabelle Linton, who go to our school. I'd pretend the comments people were making about me were jokes . . laugh and show them what a good sport I was . . make it seem like I'm not offended and that it's okay for them to make inappropriate remarks. I'd do it because after they left, Mr. Earnshaw would come over to me and put his arm on my shoulder. He'd roll his eyes at the guests walking out the door and tell me what inconsiderate asses he thought they all were.

I won't play along for Hindley.

I'm content with sulking in the corner and giving pissed-off nods to anyone who attempts to offer their bullshit sympathy. One of them is coming up to me now . . an old woman with silver hair seeking me out from halfway across the room. I recognize her from one of the dinner parties Mr. Earnshaw threw a few months back . . the wife of some business associate whose sour expression would be hard to tell apart from the rest except for the size of the diamonds that cover her fingers.

—Excuse me— she says . . her hand held out to me, holding an empty wineglass. I take a deep breath . . prepare to go
through with the unpleasant ritual of placing her hand against
my lips. As soon as my fingers touch hers, though, she pulls
away. —Just take the glass, if you don't mind— she snaps.

I lean back . . my forehead wrinkled in confusion.

She laughs through her nose . . a horrible snorting sound
as she tilts her head half around to look at the woman next to
her before turning back to me in disapproving awe. —It is
your job, isn't it?—

—Huh?— I ask.

—Well, you are one of the caterers, aren't you?— answering my question with her own.

It's so unbelievable that I'm speechless.

The women both shake their heads in a way that's familiar to me. I've seen that look so many times . . the one that
assumes I'm lazy because my eyes are dark and my skin is
always tanned.

She hands me the glass without a word . . my fingers taking it automatically as hers release their grip. I start squeezing it tighter as she starts walking away . . feel the fire
kicking in behind my eyes as I try to fight off the words that
are forming inside me. If Catherine were standing next to
me, I'd be able to stop . . I'd be able to take one or two deep
breaths and let it roll off me. But I'm alone . . my hand isn't
holding hers . . I'm only holding a dirty glass that so easily
shatters when I throw it to the floor.

A silence falls over the room after the splinters of glass
settle in their place. The old woman covers her mouth . . a

terrified look in her eyes like she's come face-to-face with some mass murderer. It's a second or two before the whispering starts. —That's the boy he took in . . I told him it was a mistake— things like that as I grind my teeth to keep from doing anything worse.

Hindley's furious. I can see it in the way he looks in my direction . . fighting his way through the crowd to get at me before I make another scene. He has his hands in the air . . telling everyone —It's nothing. It's okay— trying to lull them back to sleep . . keeping his voice calm, but the way his face is burning a bright shade of red betrays his real emotions. He seizes me by the jacket and growls —What the hell's wrong with you?— shaking me . . then slams me into the corner before turning to the petrified woman who's acting as if I'd attacked her. —I'm terribly sorry, Mrs. Andrews. He's going through a rough time. We all are— he says, trying to smooth it over with his lawyer voice. She says she understands . . says she accepts his apology, without offering her own to me.

—I hate this— I mumble as he pulls me into the kitchen.

—You have any idea who that is?— he asks and I shake my head . . tell him she obviously didn't have any idea who I was and I figure that makes us even. He's about to give me an education in names . . ready to drill them into me with his fists when Frances interrupts . . her voice all in a panic as she tells him some of the guests have started to leave . . glaring at me to let it show she obviously thinks their departure is my fault.

—Good— I mumble. —This isn't supposed to be a party—

Frances narrows her eyes and lets out her breath slowly

to warn me to stay quiet but I'm not afraid of her. She's just some whiny girl who wants to be just like them. —You watch your place— she says, wagging her finger at me.

—Go die— I whisper under my breath . . but loud enough for her to hear and she grabs her swollen belly with one hand . . raising the other dramatically to her forehead. She's the queen of exaggeration. She's been doing this since they got here. Whenever she doesn't like something, she uses her pregnancy as a way to make people bend . . making it seem like not getting her way is somehow going to hurt the baby. It's crap, of course, but Hindley buys into it. He shakes me roughly for a second time and it seems to satisfy her. She retreats again, wearing a fake smile as she tries to hold on to the popularity our dad's death is providing her.

—If you can't control yourself, why don't you at least make yourself useful?— Hindley says once she's left the room.

—By taking people's dishes?— I ask . . thinking he must be as crazy as his wife if he thinks I'm doing any of that.

—I meant, why don't you go upstairs and get Catherine to make an appearance? I think it's only appropriate— he says. It's been pissing him off all afternoon that she hasn't come down at all. She has an even harder time dealing with this than I do. To see all these people pretending to miss our father makes me angry . . but it hurts Catherine.

—Why don't you go?— I ask.

—Because she won't listen to me and you know it— he says. —For some reason, she'll listen to you— And I can tell it repulses him. He can't stand that we get along the way we do. It's the only reason I agree . . just because I know it

24

bothers him so much. Besides, it gets me away from all of them. I'd rather be with Catherine anyway.

—Make sure she's down here to say good-bye as people leave— he says as I head out of the room, on my way up the stairs. I take a quick glance into the living room, where things have returned to normal. I have no intention of trying to get Catherine down here. None of those people deserve to see her. The sooner they leave, the better. Good riddance to all of them as far as I'm concerned.

⊱ ⊰

I sit in the window and watch a parade of people shuffling out of our house. All of them dressed in black so that they look like a line of ants scattered over the sidewalk. I try to decide if they're sad just by watching the way they walk. Most of them aren't, though. Their clothes are the only thing sad about them.

I don't want to go down there. I know they're all whispering about me. Thinking I'm such a spoiled princess, hiding away in her tower. Hindley's been up here four times already, begging me to come down. I haven't opened my bedroom door for him. I haven't even spoken a word to him. I've just listened as he talked from the hallway in a tone of voice that was telling me to stop being childish. I think what he's doing is childish, though. Pretending to be nice to all those people who didn't even know Daddy.

"It's what we're supposed to do, Cathy!" he said the last time. He banged his hand on the door when he finished, to make his point, I guess. The worst part is that I know he's right. I know it's what is expected of me. They all want to see me wearing pink eyes

and sobbing. It's my role. The part I need to play so they can pity me and make the whole day complete. It should be so easy to do. It's what everybody does. I don't know why, but there's something wrong with me that keeps me from doing it.

I hear him climbing the stairs again.

He's going to try one last time to get me to cooperate before everyone leaves.

When he knocks on my door, it's softer than the last time. But trying a nicer approach won't work, I still don't want to listen.

"Go away!" I shout.

"It's me."

Henry.

I get up and hurry across the room to unlock the door. He's leaning against the frame when I open it. The dark strands of his hair hang in front of his eyes and he's smiling. Not like a happy smile, though. His smile is more of a question asking me how I'm doing. I answer by pulling him into my room and closing the door behind him, closing off the rest of the world.

He's the only one I want to see. I know he loved Dad just as much. Maybe even more because Dad didn't have to love Henry the way he had to love me and Hindley. So that love means more. One that's a choice. And that means he knows how I feel. More than any of the guests downstairs.

"Is it as bad down there as I think it is?" I ask him.

"Worse."

"I thought so," I sigh, falling backward onto my bed.

Henry sits down next to me. He's watching the birds out the window. His eyes follow them as they swoop and rise. And it's nice to be so close that we can touch hands if we need to, letting

26

time pass separate from us. It spins along as we stay still, watching the sun sink below the cliffs in the distance.

"Henry? Have you ever thought about Heaven?" I ask. "Have you ever thought you could see it? Even for only a second?"

He turns away from the window and looks at me. He watches the rise and fall of my chest for a moment before leaning back. Waits until our bodies are side by side on the bed before speaking. "Sometimes," he says and I ask him what he thinks it's like. "I think it's probably a lot like the sun."

"Maybe," I say. "Or maybe just the light. Like when we die, we become like the sun, shining to make people smile."

"Maybe," he says.

Then we don't say anything until the shadows have crawled all the way to the other side of the room. We're both too busy wondering why we're not smiling if it's true. Why isn't my dad shining on us now? Why do we only feel lost now that he's gone?

"I miss him," I say.

"Me too," he says. "But everything happens for a reason. That's what he always told us. I don't know what it could possibly be, but I guess we should trust him, you know?"

"Yeah," I say, sounding like I'm far away.

I always believed my dad when he said there was a reason for everything. I always try to make sense of things that way. It's what he taught me to do. I can't make much sense of him leaving us alone, though. Unless it's his way of telling us it's time to grow up.

I know what I need to do. I can't be a child anymore. I need to go downstairs and thank people for coming. It's what we both need to do. We need to be responsible. But before we do, I need to hear Henry say he'll do it with me. I won't let myself grow up if he doesn't grow with me. He's all I have now and I won't let him leave me too.

I push myself up on my elbows so that I'm above him. My eyes staring directly into his so that there's no way for his thoughts to wander. I push the long strands of my hair away and tuck them behind my ear before I lick my lips and swallow so that I know my mouth will form the right words. "Henry? Promise me that you'll stay with me so we can find out what Heaven's like together?"

"I promise," he says. Then he takes my hand so that I know he means it. Everyone else might leave me sometime somewhere, but not him. I will always have him.

THREE

The flowers aren't arriving anymore and the ones that were sent have already wilted. Life is starting again today. Catherine and I are going back to school. It's been more than two weeks since we've been there. It's time. I can't say I'm looking forward to it, though .. the smell of old socks in the gym locker room .. all the annoying conversations echoing through the halls .. teachers rambling on and on .. but I guess things will at least feel back to normal .. or getting there anyway.

Catherine and I can get back to normal too. Our private world together will start again. She'll belong only to me and I won't have to share her anymore. We can take our long walks through the park .. talk about feeling like fish or birds or anything else that comes to mind. We'll hold hands when we say those things and it will feel like it used to .. not like it has since the funeral.

Lately it's like Catherine thinks everything needs to change now that we're alone .. that we need to change. She hasn't said so, but there're little things that give it away. Like when she let go of my hand during the funeral .. pulled hers away from mine quickly, almost like she thought we were doing something wrong. Last night too, she turned away from me when we were lying on her bed watching the sunset like we've always done. I know they're only little things, but they mean a lot. It's like she doesn't think we should be so close anymore.

I want to tell her that I think we should be closer.

I don't know, maybe I'm making it all up, though. Maybe she just needs some time. Or maybe it's just Hindley getting to her .. all the looks he flashes at her each time he catches us doing something he considers inappropriate. Whatever it is, I'm sure it's only temporary. Once everything's back to normal, we'll be back to normal too.

—Stop thinking so much— I tell my reflection as I stare into the mirror .. concentrating on tying a perfect knot in my tie. I'm out of practice. I don't get it right until the fifth try. I pull the sweater over my head and my school uniform is complete .. run my hands through my hair and that's it. I slip my baseball cap into my backpack and sling it over my shoulder. I take one last look and tell myself —Everything's going to be fine—

As soon as I enter the hallway, I can hear Catherine in her room. She's in there with our friend Nelly. Her door's closed but I can still hear them chatting and laughing and it makes me breathe easier . . makes me think maybe I'm right and maybe everything will be fine from now on.

I want to go in there so bad . . to be part of anything that makes her laugh like that. I want to be a part of her happiness but I keep myself from knocking. She gets weird sometimes when I get too possessive and I don't want to spoil anything. There'll be plenty of time for us to be together.

Making my way down the stairs, I hear Hindley and Frances talking two floors below me . . their whispers drifting easily, spiraling around the staircase. A conspiracy of silently spoken words that are meant to be kept secret . . that would have remained secret if even one car had been driving along the avenue at just the right time or if I'd made one step noisier than the others.

Catherine is safe from their secrets. They only travel to my ears like ghosts moving behind the walls. I listen long enough to know that when I walk into the kitchen, I'll be walking into an ambush.

—You're not going to allow them to stay like that, are you?— Frances asks. I can sense her familiar expressions in everything she says . . the way she shakes her head in disgust . . the way her forehead wrinkles when her eyes roll back. —I can't believe your father ever let it get to this— she says . . each syllable spoken with a sharp sound.

I hear Hindley groan. —I'm dealing with it— he says . . saying it with a stern tone, the way he always says things when he isn't in the mood for an argument.

—Well, you'd better deal with it soon. That boy's a bad

influence on her— This coming from Frances, who's unlik-able in every way.. the kind of person who would do the world good if she suddenly evaporated, leaving behind only a skeleton. I've never understood why people like her and Hindley get to live and good people die. —God knows what the two of them do up there. Can you imagine? A boy like him in the same room with your sister.. it's disturbing— Frances doesn't bother holding her voice down. It's almost like she wants me to hear.. or Catherine maybe. Like her opinions would matter to us anyway?

—Damn it, Frances! I said it's taken care of!— Hindley shouts as a chair slides across the floor.. the angry sound of his fist striking the table, causing the dishes to vibrate and make music like the song of an earthquake.

A nervous feeling creeps into the pit of my stomach as I start down the steps again. Catherine would say I'm being crazy to worry. We both know Hindley's only barking most of the time. He rarely bites. But it's easier for her to ignore it. Hindley doesn't hate her. He hates me.. enough to try and go through with some threat. He always has. He's always thought I stole his sister away from him.. his dad too.. that I was stealing everything from him because I was a —dirty Mexican thief— and he promised to get back at me someday.

I figured he'd gotten over it after he left for college. But it's been creeping back in for the past two weeks.. ever since he showed up on the porch like he owned the place. It's something about the look in his eye.. something like a snake when he looks at me and I wonder if he ever forgot about any of it or if he's just been waiting for this moment.

I take a deep breath when I walk into the kitchen and see he's already left the room. It's a relief not having to deal with him. Frances is sitting at the table but she never even looks up from the parenting book she's reading.. one of a hundred she's read since they got here. She reads those baby books everywhere she goes just in case her swollen belly isn't enough to get attention.

I roll my eyes as I take a bowl from the cupboard. I go to the refrigerator for milk just as Hindley walks back into the room.

—What are you doing?— he asks.

I ignore him.. get the cereal out and pour the milk. He asks again.. getting up so close to me that I feel his words on my skin.

—I asked you a question—

—God.. I'm just getting breakfast— I mumble.

He grabs me suddenly by the sleeve in a burst of violence. It startles me enough to drop the bowl. I watch it fall to the floor in one piece as he twists the fabric of my sweater in his hands.. shifting the collar of my shirt so that it strangles just the tiniest bit. —Wiseass— he growls.. shoving me hard against the cabinets. —I mean what are you doing wearing that school uniform?—

—What do you mean?— I ask, struggling in his grip. I have no idea what he's talking about and don't really care. I just wish he'd take his wife and get the hell back to Los Angeles where I'll never have to think about him again.

—You're not going anywhere unless I say so— Hindley tells me.. raising his voice.. slamming his fist on the counter for the second time this morning.. causing the dishes to rattle again. It excites Frances enough to take her eyes away from the baby book. The greedy expression on her face makes her seem even less attractive than usual.. makes her beady eyes grow too large and her thin lips disappear.

Both of them suck so much! I swear, I won't last much longer with them staying here.

When Hindley finally does speak, he doesn't yell. His anger has been replaced with something else.. cruel but calm.. the same slithering meanness that he used to use when he tried to get me into trouble when we were kids.. a tattletale voice.. the kind of voice that loves to give bad news and smile at the reaction it gets. —You won't need that uniform for school anymore—he says. —I canceled your tuition— A small smile splitting his face in half when he tells me —You've been enrolled in public school—

—What? You can't do that— I shout even though I know it's what he wants. He wants me to react this way.. to get upset.. to kick and scream and everything. That's why he sprang it on me like this.. waiting until the last minute.

—I can do whatever I want!— he says.. raising his voice back at me and I can tell he's been looking forward to this confrontation. He's probably planned it out down to the very syllable. —I'm your legal guardian and I'll decide what's best—

The longer strands of my hair hang like black fog in front of my eyes, hiding every feeling of hatred I have for him. But it's getting harder to hide the more he pushes. I've put up with it so far because Catherine asked me to.. because she wanted the family to get along. No more, though. This is too much . . trying to screw up our lives like this! I don't know who he thinks he is . . marching in here after being gone for five years and he thinks he owns the place . . thinks he owns us. He thinks he knows what's best for us?

Bullshit!

He doesn't know anything about anything. Nothing about what's best for me and Catherine anyway.

—We don't need you. We can take care of ourselves— I say . . meaning for it to come out like a roar but the words are so quiet that they nearly disappear as soon as I say them.

—Do you really think I'd ever leave her alone with you? I've seen the way you look at her with your dirty spic eyes! She's supposed to be your sister, for Christ's sake!— bumping into me as he yells . . making me stumble . . making me feel smaller and dumber than I already do.

I want to go at him so bad . . hit him so hard just once because he's never understood about water signs and earth signs . . about sun and shadows . . about me and Catherine being perfect for each other. It's never stopped him from thinking he knows what's right, though.

—You don't get to just change our lives around— I say . . saying it softly . . almost a whisper and it's like he already knows that he can . . that he can do whatever he wants and doesn't have to worry about what we want.

He laughs as I try to look away from him . . a deep laugh that comes up slow like a train in the distance before it roars past . . a laugh that he's been waiting on since the first day he saw me. It's his way of letting me know that he's finally getting back at me. —Dad never changed his will— he tells me. —He never put you in it. Never mentioned you. Me, on the other hand, he mentioned. He put me in charge of everything—

—That's not true.. that can't be true— and I feel the fight inside me fading further into nothing.. wondering how Mr. Earnshaw could have done this to me.. left me the same as if he'd put me back on the side of the road the way he found me.

—It's very true— Hindley tells me.. telling me exactly what that truth means.. how it means he can take me out of private school and out of Catherine's life. He says he can turn me out of the house if he wants because I'm sixteen but that he's not going to because he'd rather keep me around to do chores. —More like a servant than a brother— are the words he uses. —More like the way you people are supposed to be—

—You're lying— but even as the sounds slip off my tongue I know he's telling the truth. I know it had to be a mistake.. that Mr. Earnshaw never would've done this on purpose. Mistake or not doesn't make any difference.. it doesn't change anything. It can't keep Hindley from being able to ruin my life.

He's enjoying all this too.. hovering over me like he's finally won something and now humiliating me is the reward.

Well, screw him!

I won't let him see that any of this bothers me. Besides, as soon as Catherine hears about this, she'll put an end to it. She'll stand up to him. —Catherine will never let you get away with this— I say.. feeling stronger suddenly.. feeling like I can do anything as long as she's on my side.

—If she doesn't, I just get rid of you— he says. His eyes fill with a glare of victory and he actually has the nerve to put his arm on my shoulder.. telling me that he's being generous.. that at least he's letting me stay here.. that he's letting me be friends with her. —I could have the papers drawn up in a matter of hours—

—So why don't you?— shrugging his hand off of me.

He laughs.. says I'm clever enough to figure that out. —She'd just end up hating me if I did that. You're going to make her think this is your idea.. that you only ever went to private school to make Dad happy. You're going to back out of her life because if you don't.. you'll never see her again, I promise— He knows the news stuns me.. knows that keeping us even slightly apart is the only way to get at me. —Now hurry up and get ready. I've enrolled you in Bayside and it's going to take you a while to get there— his eyes lighting up like traffic lights at this special surprise.

—Bayside's all the way on the other side of the city— I argue. It's over an hour on the city bus.

—It's the one you belong in— he says. —That area's full of your kind. I thought it'd be easier for you to fit in— I make my hands into fists as he talks. He glances down and sees.. tells me to go ahead.. that it would make it that much easier for him to dump me off into foster care.

—I don't know why we can't do that anyway— Frances chimes in. I narrow my eyes at her.. making them into two dark circles that show just how much I hate her.. how dangerous I could make it for her here in this house.. a sound like the low rumble building inside me and ready to

37

strike . . ready to tell her that she's less a part of this family than I am and should just keep quiet.

Hindley sees it . . senses that I'm about to say something and his hand strikes me on the side of the head. There's a feeling like stone against my skull. The surprise of it gives the impact more strength than it really should have . . enough to make me stumble . . to make me cover my ear with both hands and bite my tongue because it's also enough to make me realize he's not playing around . . that this is for real.

Fine.

I'll play along . . for now anyway.

He stops me from storming out of the room . . holds on to my wrist until I spin around. I think about hitting him . . beating the teeth out of his head as he's smiling at me. He leans in close . . whispering words that sting my skin like rubbing alcohol . . pronouncing them clear as the sun so that I won't ever forget them. —I'll never let her end up with you. My sister deserves better than a dressed-up dishwasher—

His hand releases my arm . . sends me away with a little shove through the hallway.

Once I'm out of the room, I scream inside my head . . screaming so loud without any noise that I can feel the veins growing through my skin . . the pressure so strong behind my eyes that they feel like they'll bulge from their place if I don't stop.

I promise myself not to let him get away with this. He'll never be able to keep us apart . . me and Catherine will always find a way to be together. Nothing can keep us apart for too long.

Fate won't let it.

I won't let it!

⚡⚡

"Oh! There's something else I forget to tell you!" Nelly shouts. She gets all excited and it makes me laugh. I've missed her. Not just her like the person, but the way she is, too. I've missed the way she makes even the dumbest gossip seem so important. It's nice not being so serious all the time.

My whole life has been too serious lately.

I know it's supposed to be that way. I'm supposed to act miserable because of my dad. But I know if I sit around feeling sad, I won't ever feel better. And I want to feel better. I don't want to miss him so much and maybe if I let myself have some fun, it'll help. Maybe that's selfish but it seems to make sense. It seems to be what my dad would want. That's why I invited Nelly over this morning. I figure she could sort of ease me back into school and friends and just being me.

It's sort of working. Watching her bounce around my room is at least making me smile. Not quite as big as her smile, but it's a start. My first smile in what feels like forever.

"Well? Are you going to tell me? Or are you going to just sit there, hyperventilating like a freak?" I ask.

"Okay, I'll tell you," she says, "but you have to promise not to spaz out."

39

I take a deep breath and roll my eyes back in my head. "I promise," I say so that she can tell I don't really mean it. Not because I'm going to spaz out, just because it's so childish of her to make me promise. But Nelly doesn't care. She reaches across my bed and grabs both of my hands. I watch her fingers make a circle around my wrist. She bends my hands back and presses her palms against mine so that our fingerprints collide. It's always made me shiver when she does that. She says it's the only way we can make a promise that really matters.

"Say it again," she tells me. "Promise me you won't go nuts or something."

"Fine. I promise," I say. "Now tell me already!"

All this promise stuff is just a trick to get me excited like she is. And even though it's kind of silly, it works. The whole thing makes me extra glad that I asked her to come over. I don't know if I'd be ready for school again if she didn't. If I left it to just me and Henry making our walk along the bridge, I know we'd never make it all the way to school. We would've ended up ditching and wandering up and down the hilly streets watching the way the power lines spark against the sky when the electric buses drive by. We would've found a quiet bench and talked about flying dreams or the street signs written in Chinese. Or we would've just watched the people going in and out of office buildings. Women in business skirts and sneakers. Men in striped ties and sweat stains under their armpits. We would've made up stories about their lives that lasted years and years and it would all feel so serious that I wouldn't feel any different than I did yesterday or any yesterday since Dad died.

Nelly makes me feel different.

She makes me remember that sometimes what's most important are the stupid little games we play that seem so unimportant at the time. Like the way we make promises. Or how she knows she can get me to smile by exaggerating every rumor that is whispered to her in class.

The rumor she's about to tell me is one of seismic proportions! I can tell because her tiny eyes grow to the size of bunny eyes. The slight shakiness in her voice makes my stomach flutter when she says, "Okay." The rise and fall of her chest slows down to get her ready to spill out her secret. I slow my breathing too but I can't slow my heart. It thumps quickly. Nelly's voice gets higher as she speaks. Quicker too. And her feet start to tap on the rug as she locks her fingers in between mine.

"I heard from Stephanie, who heard from Blake, that Edgar really, really likes you!" It's like an explosion when she finishes, bending my fingers back and waiting for my expression to match hers, which it never does.

"Edgar Linton?" My voice is raised more in surprise than excitement. "My neighbor down the street?"

"Yes! Can you believe it?" Then Nelly starts spazzing the way she made me promise not to. "I freaked when I heard. Ask Stephanie! I nearly fell down right in the middle of the hall! I swear to you, I almost went down flat when she told me."

"Really?" I ask, trying to show some of the excitement she does.

"Ask Stephanie! She practically had to catch me," Nelly tells me, laughing about the whole thing.

I laugh too, but I'm not sure I mean it.

I can't tell what Nelly thinks about it. About Edgar liking me,

I mean. I don't know if she thinks it's funny or if she thinks it's great. Because I have no idea which way it's supposed to make me feel and I sort of hope she'll tell me. It's not like the idea of Edgar liking me is a joke. He's one of the cutest boys in our school. Everyone knows that. Everyone agrees about that. It's just, the idea of him liking me is kind of weird. To me it's weird anyway. I've known him since kindergarten and he's never acted like he's liked me before. Or maybe he has, but I've certainly never thought about liking him!

"What's wrong?" Nelly asks.

"What do you mean?"

I put on my best fake smile but it doesn't work. It never works with her. She knows my fake smile from my real one. That's the one problem with best friends, you can't hide anything.

"What? You don't think Edgar's hot?" Nelly asks, raising her eyebrows so that her green eye shadow makes a grass-colored rainbow around them.

"It's not that," I tell her.

I want to explain it more, but she cuts me off.

"Good! I was starting to wonder if maybe you were going super prude on me," she says and I wrinkle my forehead and sigh to let her know she's being ridiculous. "So?" she asks. "Then you totally like him, right? I mean you have to. He's completely adorable."

"I guess," I say. "But I can't ever think about him without thinking about his sister too," and a shudder goes through my spine just mentioning her.

"Isabelle?" Nelly asks.

Another shiver.

"Yeah, her! I can't stand her," I say. "I can't believe she's a freshman already, she still acts like she's five."

"Yeah, she kind of sucks," Nelly agrees. "But no one's asking if you like her. I want to know if you like her brother."

I bring my hand up to my mouth and lower my head to think. I don't know how to answer her. I start sucking on the sleeve of my shirt the way I always do whenever I'm nervous. There's only one person that I've ever really liked. I'm not sure what Nelly would say if I told her. It shouldn't be such a surprise to her but maybe she thinks it's weird or something. Or maybe it's me. Maybe I think it's weird, but it's still how I feel.

"So? Do you?" Nelly asks.

I try to stall but she doesn't let me. She grabs my hands again and holds them the way that means we have to tell each other the truth. It's a best friend rule we made up long ago.

"Well, you might think it's kind of strange," I start to say but then I know by how she's looking at me so closely that I can't tell her the truth. I can't tell her about Henry and wanting to kiss him and wanting him to kiss me back. A confession like that is way too serious for my first day back to regular life.

Nelly starts to shake her head playfully and nudge me. "And? What is it? What's kind of strange?" she asks after I've stuttered long enough trying to think up a lie that never comes to me.

"Well, it's just, it's Henry," I tell her. "Edgar and he hate each other and I don't know . . . it would be weird." It's not exactly the truth, but not a lie either. They don't like each other much at all.

"Wait! You're saying you're not interested because of what

43

Henry would think?" Nelly teases. "If you really liked Edgar, it wouldn't matter."

"It's just . . . complicated," I mumble, but it comes off like the weakest protest ever.

"It's not that complicated," Nelly says. "I mean, not unless you're in love with Henry or something." The way she says it isn't like a guess, more like she's trying to name the most impossible thing in the world, but I can feel my cheeks turning red and I turn away just in time to hide it.

I don't know why, but lately I've felt like I need to hide my feelings for Henry even more. I guess because it scares me a little how much I need him since my dad died. I've even been trying to hide it from him whenever it overwhelms me, whenever I feel closest to him. Last night I had to move away from him when we were together on my bed. I knew I wouldn't be able to stop myself if I didn't. I can't let myself do that because I'm still not convinced there isn't something wrong with me dreaming about us getting married. I've written about it in my diary for as long as I can remember. Maybe that's how I've been able to trick myself into thinking it's okay. That it's more than just a little-girl crush that I need to grow out of before it's too late.

"Well?"

"I don't know, Nelly," I say, dropping my hands into my lap and trying to make sense of everything inside of me.

"Just give him a chance!" Nelly says. "You can't let Henry be your whole life." The last part comes out louder than the rest. Too loud.

"Shhhhhhh!" I whisper, putting my finger to my mouth and hitting her with the other hand because the sound of footsteps echoes in from the hall.

"Is that him?" she whispers.

I nod and then we sit paralyzed as we listen to Henry cross the hall so that he's standing right outside my bedroom door. It feels like a game of hide-and-seek. The tension is too much and I start to giggle like crazy for no reason except that I can't sit still anymore. Nelly laughs too, more because I laughed than because she needed to. I don't think I really breathe again until I hear him going down the stairs.

"Do you think he heard?" I ask.

"Does it matter?" Nelly says. "I mean it's true after all. You got to live your life for you. So what if he doesn't like Edgar? Let him deal with that."

It's easier just to say yes than it is to say all the other things. So that's what I say. "Yeah, I guess."

"Good, because I sort of told Edgar we'd walk to school together today."

"WHAT?" I can't believe she'd do that! Well, actually I can believe it because it's exactly the kind of thing she would do. But still, today of all days! So much for easing back into anything. The entire walk to school is going to be me figuring out how to keep Henry from killing Edgar, especially if he picks up any clue that Edgar likes me.

"It'll be fun," Nelly insists.

"It most definitely won't be fun," I insist back at her.

She knows exactly what I mean by that and she grins. She's seen Henry get crazy when any boy starts chatting with me. "Well, it'll be interesting. You have to admit that."

I want to be mad at her, but I can't. She means well. But that doesn't mean I'm looking forward to this walk any more than before. She knows I'm the one who'll have to deal with it if it all blows up. I'm the one who will have to calm Henry down like always. But maybe it won't be so, so bad. At least it will give me something else to think about besides all the depressing stuff that I've had to think about for the last week or so. So I can't be too pissed off.

"Fine. Let's get it over with, then," I say.

I go over to my desk. I throw a few last things in my bag. One last check in the mirror shows that the freckles on my face have spread from my nose to my cheeks thanks to spending all day out in the sun yesterday. I make a useless wipe at them and turn away.

Nelly gets up and grabs her things. She's out of my bedroom in a flash, already halfway down the first flight of stairs before I get into the hall. I put my hand on the railing and go down the first few steps just in time to see Henry coming the other way in a hurry.

He must have forgotten something like usual.

"Better hurry up," I tease. "We're not going to wait for you if you're late." But he must not get that I'm kidding because he bumps into Nelly, nearly knocking her down before glaring up at me.

"Hey? What's the matter with you?" Nelly shouts, rubbing the soreness out of her shoulder where they collided.

"Nothing!" Henry barks.

He rushes up toward me.

I grab on to his arm and pull him to a stop. I make him turn to the side and look at me. I wish I didn't, though. He has that look in his eyes. The one where the brown almost looks orange whenever he's angry. It scares me a little. Scares me more when I think about Edgar waiting on the sidewalk three houses down and what that look in Henry's eyes might mean then.

"Just go ahead of me, okay!" Henry says. I can tell he's trying to keep from getting mean. I can hear it in the way his voice is strained.

I ask him what happened. I'm sure Hindley's said something. I know it's sucked for him with Hindley here. Not that Henry ever wants to tell me about it. He says he's old enough to fight his own battles. "Can I help?" I ask.

He tells me again to leave. "Don't wait for me either," he says. He makes his voice calm this time. He hides all the anger in his words but it's still there in the orange center of his eyes and I know him well enough to know when to let things go.

"Okay," I say. But before I leave him, I move my body next to his. The space on the stairs is so narrow and confined that it feels like we're Siamese for a second and I have to do everything I can not to kiss him right there and forget all about whatever the world might think.

I want to.

Every tiny part of me wants to and it makes the clear white hairs on my arm stand on end. My mouth so close to his that it almost happens on its own. We just barely escape when I feel him pull away from me.

"Come on!" Nelly hollers from the next floor down.

In the split second I turn my head to look at her, Henry is gone. Already up the stairs and racing toward his room. The door creaking open and then slamming closed behind him. Only a ghost of him is left standing next to me, but it's enough to keep the sparks tingling all along my skin for a moment longer before they fade.

47

Then I hurry away.

"What's his problem?" Nelly asks.

"I'm sure it's just another argument with my brother," I say. "It's kind of the routine around here." I try to make it sound like it's no big deal even though it bothers me. But I guess everybody does that, makes their family fights seem unimportant. "He said not to wait for him, though. I'm sure he'll catch up with us."

I avoid the kitchen on the way out. I don't even poke my head in to say good-bye to Hindley. I know whatever happened is his fault and I don't want to see him for the rest of the day. That's my new thing. Whenever he acts like a jerk, I'm just going to ignore him for a whole day. He probably won't care, but it makes me feel better. Even just imagining a hurt look on his face when he hears me going out the front door without a word makes me feel like I'm getting even.

As soon as we step outside, I notice that I'm dressed too warm. There's no breeze blowing in from the ocean and the sun has already burned off the morning fog. There's no need for the sweater I'm wearing. I take it off as we step off the porch. Then I shake my hair back into place. And when the world comes back into focus, I see Edgar waiting on the sidewalk.

The way he's standing, it's like he's posing for a magazine ad. He's got one hand in his pocket and the other is holding a jacket over his shoulder. He has his face turned toward the sun so that it catches the right light and makes his hair look so blond that it almost turns white. He looks so ridiculous, so full of himself, that if I didn't know better I'd think it was a joke.

Isabelle comes out of their house as we get closer.

I stop walking and cross my arms.

Her hair is styled so carefully into an uneven black bob made to look messy with the help of tons of gel and an hour of work. She makes me nauseous. Even the way she wears her school uniform makes me shake my head. It's the same as the rest of us, but she turns the collar out, ties a knot in the sleeves, anything to make it look like it's right out of the display windows in the trendiest boutiques. She thinks it makes her so great, but it all just looks so fake. She'd never know it, though. Her nose is stuck so high up in the air that she can't see what everyone thinks about her.

"Do we have to do this?" complaining one last time.

Nelly nods.

She slides her arm under mine, locks elbows with me, and I let her lead me along. I give one last look up to the windows on the fourth floor of our house. Crossing my fingers. I haven't given up hope that Henry will come to my rescue.

"Hi, Catherine," Edgar says and there's a nervous way about him as he waves. The whole picture of cool he was trying to give off is totally ruined when his voice cracks just a little as he asks me how I am.

"Fine," I say, still not willing to move beyond one-word answers.

As we start walking, Nelly moves in front with Isabelle. I hear her asking Isabelle all kinds of questions about her classes and her clothes and her friends. I don't know how she does it, but she manages to sound interested as Isabelle drones on about herself in that whiny voice of hers. Isabelle has no clue that Nelly's only pretending to care so that me and Edgar can fall back behind them.

Edgar isn't much better than his sister, though.

He keeps going on about immature pranks he and his friends

have played lately. Pulling chairs out from under people. Pantsing freshmen in gym class. Dumb things like that, so I'm barely listening. I'm too preoccupied thinking about Henry. About how we almost kissed and about how he isn't here with me to see the birds dip in and out of the last of the fog that still hangs over the Golden Gate Bridge.

Edgar can tell I'm distracted. He'd have to be a moron not to. "Catherine?" he says, trying to pull me back into his conversation.

"Hmmm," I mumble.

"Catherine," he says again. This time I look at him because the way he says my name is different from the way he's said anything to me his whole life. "I'm sorry about your dad. I didn't get the chance to tell you after the funeral, but I wanted you to know."

I tilt my head and stare at him like he's a stranger.

Suddenly it's like the whole act he's put on in front of me since we were kids just evaporates. I concentrate on his face and for the first time I think maybe there's something sweet about him under all the showing off that I never saw before.

"I mean it," he says. "I'm really sorry."

"Thanks," I say.

We start walking again, only now he stays quiet. It's like he's letting me know that he's there and that he'll listen if I want him to. It might just be my imagination, but I get the feeling that maybe he understands. And maybe that's why I reach down and take his hand. Or maybe it's because I'm wishing Henry is there instead and he's just a substitute.

I don't know.

But whatever it is, it's nice.

We start to swing arms a little as we walk and I actually smile at him. *Something about being with him makes me feel more nor-mal than I've felt in days.*

I'm sure it'll go away. We'll stop pretending once all his too cool friends see us. Sooner than that if Henry catches up with us because if I see him, I'll drop Edgar's hand faster than anything. But until then, it's kind of fun acting like someone different. Like someone who doesn't have any worries.

⚒ ⚒

The window clouds up every time I exhale. My fingers streak across it like a windshield wiper.. making a stroke with each step she takes. I keep the glass clean enough to watch her take off her sweater.. watching the soft morning light settle on her naked arms like a warm halo. Watching her makes me want to rush out and grab hold of her.. keep her so close that we both fade into each other.

I should've told her what was going on. I had the chance when we were both on the stairs.. one whisper would have told her about Hindley's attempt to create a dictatorship over our lives.

I didn't because all she could talk about yesterday was how nice it was going to be to have a normal, boring day. She's been looking forward to not dealing with the daily drama that we haven't been able to avoid. I didn't want to ruin that. She'd completely break down if I told her. She would have gone right at Hindley and had it out with him in the kitchen. I didn't want to put her through that.

It can wait until tonight.

One day won't kill me.

Besides, I know Hindley, and this isn't going to last. It will blow over once he thinks he's taught me a lesson. He'll give up once he realizes he can't keep us apart. It's the only thought that prevents me from going berserk when he starts shouting for me to hurry up.. his voice like a whip trying to make me move faster.

I tell myself again that it's only one day. —No big deal—

I finish getting out of my uniform and put on jeans.. a long-sleeve T-shirt and my baseball cap. It won't be so bad.. I just have to think of it like a field trip. I slip my phone in my pocket as I head down the stairs. I'll give Catherine a call as soon as I'm out of the house. I'll make up some excuse for not going to school.. something that won't make her worry. I'll tell her Hindley needs me to go to Dad's office and fill out some paperwork.. something that won't require a lot of explanation because I'll pretend not to understand why I have to do it. I'll promise to meet her after school.. to wait for her under the bridge and then I can tell her everything.

Hindley's waiting at the bottom of the stairs for me.. his arms folded in front of his chest, trying to look tough.. to intimidate me. But I'm not as little as I used to be. He can't push me around like he did when I was a scrawny kid.

—She's gonna know this is all you— I warn him as I try slipping past.

—Not if you tell her otherwise— he says.

—Why would I do that?— I mumble.

He doesn't answer.. just tells me to give him my phone. He says I'm no longer entitled to such luxuries. —You've lost all phone privileges— he says as I take the phone from my pocket.

—You think I'll go along with this just so I can have a cell phone?— I ask. It's the kind of bribe only someone as spoiled as Hindley could think up. Like I'm going to give up the most important person in my life for a piece of plastic.

—No . . not exactly— he says. —It's getting disconnected. But not until Catherine gets a text from you. Don't worry, it'll explain everything to her . . all your reasons for wanting to transfer away from those hypocrites at your school. She knows you've never liked them, so it won't be hard to believe. The harder part will be when you tell her that you think the two of you need space. Don't worry, I'll do my best to make you sound convincing—

—How could you do that?— I ask . . not thinking about me or about hating him . . I'm thinking about her instead . . about how he's punishing her the same as me. —It's going to hurt her feelings—

Hindley takes two quick breaths and twists the side of his mouth up in concern. —It might— he says, pretending to care. —But it would be worse for her if I was to take you away from her altogether. You know it too, that's why you're going to put up with this. Then you'll see in the long run that this is what's best for her—

I get so angry listening to him that my skin burns. Every inch of me wants to hit him . . wanting the feeling of his bones shattering under my fists. But I know it would be even worse for her if I lose my temper.

—You won't get away with this— I say.

He steps aside then, showing me the door. —We'll see— he says and tells me to run along, like giving a command to a dog.

I rush past him and out the front door. My brain already swimming with ideas on how to get out of this mess..snippets of schemes that so far aren't adding up to much, but they will. They have to.

I catch the bus heading toward the Bay Bridge..sliding through the aisle past the other passengers..row after row of them until the bus drives away from the curb. I stumble forward when the engine jerks into motion. I grab the bar above my head and gain my balance..wander more to the back and fall into an empty seat where I can press my forehead against the window.

The sun pokes through the buildings..disappears as the bus rolls downhill..reappears up the next. I watch it and remember what Catherine tells me to do whenever everything inside me gets so knotted up with anger. I remember to focus on the white center of the sun and close my eyes. —*Keep the sun on the tip of your nose and breathe..in and out real slow and think about something that makes you happy*— I can almost hear her voice saying it as the bus drives on.

I never tell her that she's what I think about..that it's her and not the memory of the sun sitting on the tip of my nose that makes me relax.

I picture the way she stands when she gets out of bed in the morning..stretching her arms above her head..the thin muscles in her shoulders and the slight curve of her breasts showing through her nightshirt..the easy way in which her body goes soft when her arms come down to her sides. I think about the way her voice sounds during the sunrise when she says —*Good morning, Henry*— The harder I think about her, the quicker my anger rots away like burn holes spreading through paper.

She's says that's part of being a Pisces too.. the way my emotions can shift and change like the tides being pulled by the moon. They can change as often as waves.. one mood replaced as quickly as it came.

I keep my eyes closed and drift along.. block after block.. minute after minute. It doesn't seem so terrible anymore.. doesn't seem so hopeless as the bus grinds to a stop.

Bayside High School is waiting as I step off.. a crumbling gray building decorated with spray paint tags like Christmas lights on a dead tree. As I walk up the front steps I begin to feel like a kind of fish that needs air to breathe but the surface is so far above my head that my fins can never swim there.. spinning them in mad circles as I struggle.. because that's how today is.. that's how it feels with everything changing so fast.. like maybe every particle of dust in the universe has turned against me for some reason.

Everything except her, I mean.

There's always Catherine to keep me going.

I just need to hang in there and eventually she'll make this all go away.

FOUR

By the time Nelly comes up to me after last period, I feel like a zombie walking through the halls. Everyone else seems to be passing me like I'm stuck in slow motion. I haven't been able to get up to their speed all day. Like I'm going through the motions but I'm not really here.

Without Henry, I feel out of place. The classrooms look the same. The desks are in the same spots as they've always been. The same kids are in each class. The sunlight shines through the windows the same as it has since sixth grade, but it feels unfamiliar to me. I know it's because he's missing. I've missed him in every hallway at the start and end of every period. I miss knowing that wherever I turn, he'll be smiling from the door of some other classroom.

I missed him during lunch when everybody was asking me about my dad. He would've found the right words to answer their questions. I mess up things like that. I say too much, or too little, or just things that don't make any sense. I need him in those situations. I need just knowing he's on my side no matter what stupid things I say. Things come out better when I know he's there with me.

I miss the way his eyes look like the two brightest lights in the world shining just for me. The way the left side of his mouth curls up in a silly smile that he's only ever let me see. The way his hair looks like the ocean at midnight. I miss everything about him because it's like part of me is missing. Like a hole has been cut through me as easily as cutting paper and I've felt that kind of empty all day.

Just drifting like a balloon without a hand holding its string.

But I miss him the most right now because this is always the time of day when the rest of the world vanishes. I'm almost afraid of leaving. Walking home without the feeling of my hand lost inside his palm scares me more than anything.

"Catherine!" Nelly calls out as she hurries toward my locker. "I've been looking for you since lunch," she says, trying to catch her breath. "I just heard about Henry. He transferred? Why?"

I hug my books close to me and shrug.

It's better to pretend that I don't know than to tell the truth. That it's because of me. It's my fault he thinks we should be apart. "We need some space." That's how he put it but what he really meant was that he needed space from me. I've been too emotional with him. Showing too much of how I feel about him. I know I have. I've been trying to hold back but I guess it was still too much. At least now I know he doesn't feel the same way about me.

"Did you call him?" Nelly asks.

I nod. "At least ten times," I admit. "He didn't answer."

Nelly leans against the locker next to mine. She sighs and tilts her head back, trying to figure out some way it all makes sense. "That's probably why he was so weird this morning," she says.

"Probably," I mumble.

The halls begin to thin out. Fragments of conversation are left behind for a moment before the voices follow their owners outside. It's lonelier without the comforting chatter. The silence only reminds me that I have to go home eventually and face him. It's not going to be easy watching him dance around what really bothers him. When he rejects me, I just hope his eyes don't give away that he thinks I'm a freak for ever falling in love with him.

Nelly asks me what I'm going to do and I tell her I don't know. Then she offers me a way out, asking, "Do you want to come over?" I'm ready to accept when she tells me, "No. Wait. I promised my mom I'd go shopping with her today," she says, making it sound like the most unappealing chore in the world. "You can come, if you want."

"No thanks," I say. "I'm not in the mood for crowds."

"That's cool. Besides, I'm sure it'll all be fine," faking a smile as she says it.

"Yeah, I'm sure," I say, not even trying to fake one.

I take out the books I don't need from my bag and replace them with ones I do need from my locker. Nelly waits with me even though we'll be going separate ways as soon as we step outside. She'll head for the bus that will take her to meet her mom and I'll turn for the bridge where I'm going to miss Henry the most as I walk.

"Don't look now, but here comes your boyfriend," Nelly teases as I'm closing my locker. She points with her eyes to the end of the hall. I glance over my shoulder and see Edgar walking right for us.

I'm not really in the mood for his company. I'd rather be alone, but it's not fair to tell him that. He was so nice to me this morning and everything. It would be too mean to ignore him.

He waves once he sees he's been spotted.

"Hi," I say, waving just with my fingers without smiling.

"Hey, you heading home?" Edgar asks once he's next to me. "Do you mind if I walk home with you?" he asks after I nod. He's shuffling his feet nervously. I can see his fingers tapping his leg as they hide in his pocket and his eyes grow wide like a little boy on a roller coaster.

"Guess not," I say.

"Gotta go," Nelly says, winking at both of us. It makes Edgar blush and he hides his head by looking down at his shoes. It's actually kind of sweet and I feel the start of a smile. I don't let it grow, though. There're too many other things on my mind to let myself smile.

Nelly makes a gesture as she leaves. Her lips mouth for me to call her later. Mine mouth back to her that I will. It might be a lie, though. It depends on how terrible my evening goes. If Henry breaks my heart the way I'm thinking he's going to, I won't be talking to anyone.

Edgar lets me lead the way, following me onto the campus and across the lawn. I fold my hands together behind my back, watching the way my shoes make little clouds of dust once we reach the path that runs along the bay. I peek at him every few steps, but he's not looking at me. He's looking at the sky. At the trees. Anywhere except at me. Sometimes I see his mouth start to move, trying to think of things to say but never actually saying anything because I keep moving ahead silently.

He must think I'm so weird, but I can't help it.

I don't feel much like talking.

I watch the birds instead. It's beautiful how they glide in front of the sun. Sometimes I can feel their shadows move over me. It's only for a second before they fly off, disappearing in the branches. There's no sign of them after. Only the rustling of leaves and the faint impression of warmth returning to my skin. It all seems less special having them all to myself. Henry would smile at me if he saw me watching them. He would hold my hand and then I would laugh. His eyes would light up a softer shade of brown as we talk about the secret way that birds communicate with each other and how it's sort of like the way we have a secret language. Those are the things that make it beautiful watching birds fly. There's nothing mysterious about it without him. They're just frightened pigeons.

We reach the top of the hill and Edgar clears his throat. He pretends ten minutes of silence have never passed. It's fine with me. It shows at least that it hasn't bothered him. "How was your first day back?" he asks.

"Okay," I mumble, twisting the fingers of my one hand with the fingers of my other, wondering how honest I can be with him. "Actually it was kind of strange," I say, deciding it doesn't matter what he thinks. I just need to tell someone. "It felt like everyone was staring at me and acting weird because my dad died."

"Probably no one wanted to say anything that might upset you by accident," he says.

"Yeah," I say. Everyone was so careful about what they said to me today. Even my teachers kept apologizing for no reason. I know they're just trying to be nice, but it makes me feel so claustrophobic. That's where I needed Henry most. "I wish they wouldn't," I admit to Edgar. *"It's like the more people treat me like I'm going to break apart, the more I feel like I need to, you know?"*

I turn away from him as soon as I finish. The last echo of my voice ripples over the bay and I'm embarrassed by the way it all came out like that. He doesn't even know me. I guess maybe that's what made it so easy.

I stop walking and stare into the distance at the buildings. I let the wind blow my hair in front of my eyes so he won't notice that I'm starting to break apart right now. He notices anyway, though, putting his hand on my elbow.

"Hey, don't worry about it," he says.

"I'm sorry." I feel so stupid. We're not even friends, let alone close enough friends for me to blab away at things that he doesn't want to hear. "Today was just hard, that's all."

"It's no problem," he says. "I get it."

"You do?"

"Well, sort of anyway. I won't pretend to know how you feel or anything. But I get it that it's annoying when people treat you like you're a freak or something," he says and I realize that he really does get it. It makes me feel better. Makes me feel less alone.

"Thanks," I say.

"What for?"

"I don't know," I say, smiling easier now. "Just for talking to me, I guess." He's the only one who's been honest with me all day.

⊱⊰

I made it through the day by not saying a word..not looking anyone in the eye..doing nothing that would give anyone a reason to take notice of me because Bayside High isn't the kind of school I want to stand out in. It's hardly a school at all..more like a prison the way there're steel gates on the windows and metal detectors at the doors. It's nothing like Academy with its open campus and view of the water. There're no computer labs..no student lounges with sofas and coffee for sale..no restaurant chains in the cafeteria..nothing that I'm used to. But those aren't the things that make it so unfriendly. It's the kids that go there..walking through the halls like wolves in packs.. wild and dangerous like all they've ever learned is how to be tough.

Like those idiots after last period, blocking my way and pretending not to notice that I was trying to get by..wanting me to bump into them so they'd have an excuse to beat the shit out of me. They thought they were being so smart but it's all just so predictable and pointless..testing the new kid to see how tough I am. They're just as brain-dead as the clones who attend private school..behaving exactly the way the world expects them to.

Idiots.

I lowered my shoulder and pushed through. All four of them started barking at me right away..throwing their arms out and calling me back as I kept going..saying I was a pussy and promising that they'll still be waiting there for me tomorrow.

Whatever.

I won't let myself get sucked into that shit. It's what Hindley wants..what he expects to happen by sending me here. He wants me to get as wild as those kids who go around punching people in the head for kicks. It would prove that he's been right about me all along.

I won't let that happen.

I won't change no matter what he does.

Catherine and I won't change either. We'll still spend the afternoons alone in her room watching the sunset through the window. None of that's going to change just because I'm at a different school.

She's probably worried about me. God knows what Hindley told her while he was pretending to be me. Nothing that can't be undone as soon as I get home. As soon as I explain everything to her, it's going to backfire on Hindley.. he's going to be the one she pulls away from.. she might even be able to get him to go back to L.A.

The bus seems to hit every red light going through the city.. inching along with regular stops on every other corner.. people taking their time getting on and off. It takes forever to get back to the Heights.. for the crowded buildings to give way to homes with a little space between their walls.. for the parking meters to bloom into trees and the gasoline smell of traffic smog to start smelling like the salt air of the ocean. But it finally does.. the bus begins to slow for the last time.. the engine shifts and the brakes grind down. When the doors open, I step into the fresh air with the city at my back, sitting lower on the horizon.. the steeple roof of our house in front of me.

I keep staring at her window as I walk.. hoping for a glimpse of her watching out for me.. for any sign that she's missing me as much as I'm missing her. There's no sign of her by the time I reach the porch but it doesn't worry me. It only makes me want to see her more . . to rush up the stairs and find her curled up on her bed. I'll walk slowly to her side . . my face like an apology as I wait for her to smile before I tell her everything.

The snap of a newspaper from the nearest room greets me as I walk through the front door. I see that it's Frances, so I hold in my smile as she holds out a piece of paper toward me. —Here— she says, shoving the note in my face.

I grab at it . . crumpling it into a ball when I notice Hindley's handwriting. —What's this?— I ask.

—I thought you would've learned to read by now— Frances says . . her eyes faking genuine surprise. I ignore her and unfold the piece of paper . . smooth it out on my leg . . let letters untangle themselves into words before I can read it.

I have to read it twice before it makes any sense . . a third time before I even get what it's telling me to do . . several more times after that before I understand all the consequences of what it really means.

—There're some boxes up there already— Frances says, responding to Hindley's note demanding that I move my stuff into the basement. —You're going to have to make a lot of trips—

She seems to enjoy the shocked expression on my face . . telling me I might want to clean up the basement a little first . . running through a list of things that need to be done to make it livable . . saying each one with a smile like she's going over a list of gifts instead of a list of chores.

—Where's Catherine?— I ask .. listening for any sound of her coming to my rescue like she's done so many times when me and Hindley are fighting.

—Not home— Frances says. —She's with that boy Edgar .. I think you know him, right?— Her face twists into a smile when she mentions him .. trying to make me believe Catherine is together with that jerk .. hoping that it will bother me but I'm not buying it. Catherine can see right through people like that. If she's really even with him at all, she's only doing it to be polite. —It's nice to know she'll have him to turn to once we send you away for being such a pain in the ass—

I don't take the bait.

I'm not going to lose my temper and give her any reason to get rid of me sooner.

—Fine— I mumble. I'll take a box of stuff down there to the basement .. maybe even two or three .. but then Catherine will come home and it'll end the same as always. She'll be on my side and Hindley will crawl away like a sore loser.

The boxes are on the floor outside my room right where Frances said they'd be. I pick one of them up .. carry it over to my desk and toss some things in it .. things that will be easy to put back. I take them to the room in the basement that shares a wall with the laundry room. There's a damp smell of swamp water and stains on the cinder blocks from the last rain. I switch on the light in the spare room and the bulb flickers to life .. blinking against a mattress sitting in the middle of the room .. already a stack of folded sheets laid out for me to make it up as a bed. I shake my head at how far Hindley's willing to take this .. as if I'm actually going to spend even one night down here where mice leave their droppings tucked into every corner.

The second trip is easy too. So is the third and fourth . . taking some stuff that had been lying on my floor. But the fifth time I go up there, I need to start taking things out of drawers or closets . . things that aren't supposed to move. I don't want to start with that stuff. It'll make it more difficult to act like the whole thing isn't happening . . make it feel less like a joke. I empty the fourth box onto the mattress . . watch as its contents spill over onto the thin rug that covers the cement floor like drops of water dripping into a bucket that is getting full. Each item that tumbles out makes me a little angrier and I wonder what's keeping Catherine.

I start to breathe easier when I hear the front door open.

I turn to the stairs, leaving the box where it fell. I'll only need it for carrying things back up again.

—Catherine?— I call out when I'm on the first floor . . calling her again when there's no answer as I head into the kitchen. Hindley's there . . waiting when I come through the door. I stay where I am . . watch as he takes the suit jacket off his shoulders and drapes it over a chair . . undoes the band of his watch and lays it gently on the table before loosening the tie under his collar.

—I see you've already started . . that's good— he says without glancing at me. I keep my mouth shut as he moves from the table to the counter . . gliding automatically like the buses along the electric lines. He places his briefcase on the flat surface . . a sudden snapping of the locks as they flip open. He shuffles through some folders and papers . . removes a stapled stack of something official looking and hands it to me.

The state seal of California is printed clearly across the top. I skim through the first few lines and hand it back to him. —What's this supposed to be?— I ask.

—Proof— he says.

—Of what?—

—That I mean what I say— Hindley tells me. —Those are documents authorizing your transfer back into state care. All they require is a signature from me and about a week of processing. After that . . adios, Henry— he says with a wave and smile.

I watch the papers drop to the counter and suddenly realize just how much control he has over me.

—No smart-ass comment to make?— he asks and I stay quiet. —Well, that's for the best. You got a lot of work to do. I want your crap out of that room before Catherine gets home. I don't want her throwing a fit and trying to stop me. She won't be able to . . you know that, right? Not this time . . she's not going to save you like some stray . . it won't work like it always did with Dad—

Every part of me feels numb . . feels like my bones have dissolved into powder because this time he might really win.

Hindley takes a glass from the cupboard . . pours himself a drink and waves the papers in front of me. —She's not going to know about this— he says. —She's going to keep running to you, so you'll need to push her away if you want to stay here. Got that?—

I nod like a dog that I understand . . like a dog that's been kicked but will wait for the right moment to bite back. I'll do what he says for now since it seems to be the only way to stay close to her. I'd rather keep nearby. . planning and waiting for a time to get back at him. But I also know I need to come up with something quick because I won't survive long without being at her side.

For now, I have to do what he says.

I finish moving the rest of my stuff, doing my best to ignore the way Catherine seems to be all around me each time I go onto the top floor of the house. . her smell lingering like a ghost that makes me realize exactly how much I'm losing.

There's no trace of her in the basement.

No sunlight trickling in through the windows like it would from her room. There's nothing down here except my junk, which doesn't mean anything to me. And it's hours before I hear the sound of her steps on the porch. . hear her call my name. She disappears as quick as she came. . up one floor and another before I have the chance to answer.

It doesn't take long after for the shouting to start. Her voice and Hindley's competing for space. . fighting over me. . one for me and the other against. Then there's a reverse in direction and she's running back down. . running to me. . to find me sitting in here like another stain in the scenery.

She comes into the room and I can't bring myself to look at her. I'm too embarrassed. . feel too much like an idiot. She wants to know why I didn't tell her this morning but I don't feel like explaining it anymore because it only makes me feel more like a failure. I wanted to show her I could take care of myself so that she'd see that I could take care of her. I guess I can't do either, though.

—I would've stopped him— she says.

—I know— I say.. leaning back to look up at the beams that crisscross the ceiling.. shaking my head at how stubborn I am. Hindley never would've had those papers made up if I'd told her this morning what was going on. But he has them now. He won't give them up now.. it would've had to be then and I screwed it all up.

Catherine tells me that it will all blow over once Frances has the baby. She says they'll lose interest in me.. that they might even pack up and leave us alone together. I agree with her only because I don't want her feeling worse than she already does. But I know none of it's true. Catherine's never hated anyone in her life.. she can't understand how much Hindley hates me. I understand, though.. enough anyway. He's wanted this too long to give up. He'll never get bored with doing this to me.

—He'll never be able to split us up. I promise— she says.

Her face is right next to mine.. the smell of vanilla on her lips.. traces of sunset dust in her hair. She has no idea that he's already split us up.. even if it's just a crack.. even if it's just the fourth floor to the basement, it's something and cracks are hard to repair.. cracks only get wider.

—Right? We'll always be together?— she asks and I want so bad to look away because I'm beginning to think she's wrong. But her eyes are swollen and red and I know what she needs me to say.. I know she needs me to agree and so I pretend to smile like I would if she'd asked me the same question as we were walking through the park.

—Right— I say.

She puts her arms around my neck and holds me tighter because she knows I don't mean it. I can feel the way the bones in her spine shiver as she cries.. the way her voice scratches against her throat when she talks and I wonder if Hindley realizes how much he's hurting her too.. that it's only going to make me want to get back at him even worse than I already do.

⚓ ⚓

The color of the sky changes to a deeper shade of twilight outside. It creeps into the room like a guest and it seems to make us both tired. I start to twist the ends of my hair around my finger and Edgar watches me. We run out of words to say, but even so, it's a nice kind of quiet. Normal. Sometimes I wish this is the way my family would be.

Mrs. Linton is starting to make dinner. She asks me if I want to stay. She says it's not any more difficult to set for five instead of four as she takes a stack of plates from the cabinet and places them on the counter.

Part of me wants to borrow their family for a little bit longer, but I shouldn't. "I better go," I say. Mrs. Linton looks at me through the top of her eyes; she's disappointed in me for turning down her invitation but I know she's only kidding. I smile at her, letting the curl of hair slip from my finger.

"Well, you're welcome to come back anytime," she says. Then

she looks at Edgar and back at me. "I'm sure my son would enjoy your company."

Edgar turns a slight shade of pink. "Mom, can't you leave us alone for one minute?" he says. He leans over the table to whisper. "Sorry. She's kind of a pest," he says to me, deliberately loud enough for his mother to hear.

"It's okay," I say, laughing a little.

I don't mind the way she's been hovering around us. It's sort of nice having a mom around for a change. Besides, it's kind of cute the way he gets so embarrassed. I always pictured the Lintons as being so snobby. It's good to know I was wrong. They're just like regular people. And the way things have been at home, it's nice to know there's a place I can go to get away from it if I want.

I get up from the table and Edgar stands up too. He follows me to the door. "Do you want me to walk with you?" he asks, trying to act all innocent but we both know what he means by that.

"It's only two houses away," I tell him, putting my hands on my hips. I shift my weight onto one foot and give him a little smile.

A shy smile creeps across his face and he's blushing more than before. It makes me blush a little too. "Yeah, I know," he says, tilting his head away from me. It's cute how he's been around me all afternoon. It almost makes me want to say yes, but deep down I know I don't want him to. I know he doesn't mean it. Not really. I know he'll lose interest in me after a few weeks or maybe even days. As soon as I'm not new to him anymore. That's just the way he is and we both know it. It's better if we act like it too.

"Thanks, but I'll be fine," I tell him. I see his eyes get fake-sad just before he lowers his head and lets the longer blond curls fall in front of them. I touch his hand and thank him again for being so nice to me.

He nods and does his best to look happy as I leave.

I wave to him from the sidewalk, but I'm already thinking about Henry. Each step that brings me closer makes it that much more impossible to think about anything else. The time I spent with Edgar didn't make my anxiety go away. It just made me forget about it for a little while.

Forgetting for a few hours isn't the same thing as making it go away.

The second I step inside our house, all the things I was worrying about before will sweep over me. I'll be wrapped up so tight in them that it will feel like I'm suffocating. It feels that way just imagining the things Henry will say to me. It's only going to be worse when it's his voice saying them instead of my just anticipating them. But I need to get it over with. I need to find out what's going on even if it means giving up on the idea of Henry and me living happily ever after. I can't take waiting to find out anymore. Life's too uncertain to wait. I've learned that the hard way. It's the last lesson my dad ever taught me.

As soon as I step into the house, I head straight for the top floor. The tapping of my shoes on the stairs is like the hurried pounding of my heart. I'm so scared I'm going to lose him forever. Scared enough that I'm ready to give up that part of me that wants to kiss him as long as we can still be best friends. Whatever he wants us to be, I'll do my best to make it that way.

I run my hand along the banister to keep my balance as I make the turn into our hallway. I hurry past my door, going straight for his room. His door is open. I rush forward, expecting to see him sitting at his desk or lying on the bed. He's probably waiting for this. Probably has been since this afternoon because he knew when he sent me that message that I would need more explanation.

My heart nearly stops beating when I enter his room.

Every part of me is frozen for an instant, like I've vanished along with all of his things that used to be there. I open my mouth to scream but the sound comes out empty. Any trace that Henry ever existed is gone. The small pile of his favorite books that he kept stacked neatly near his windowsill. The glass figurine of a horse in mid-gallop that I gave him for his eighth birthday has run off even though it's never galloped farther than his desk before. The Oakland A's baseball cap that he wears every day isn't resting on the handle of the closet door like it always does. The rest of the closet is empty too. Even the warm scent of rain that always stays with him is gone. Nothing's left except the furniture and dust bunnies that tumble over the floorboards.

I struggle to breathe for a second. It feels like the empty space is trying to erase me as easily as it erased him. I have to grab on to the door frame to keep myself from being destroyed by whatever horrible thing swallowed Henry.

I'm pulled back by the sound of footsteps behind me.

"Henry?" I back out of the room with my fingers crossed, hoping to see him. My voice trembles like the last fragments of shattered glass trying to stay in place. The sound of everything I've ever been afraid of all coming true at once. I turn around slowly, knowing there must be a perfectly reasonable explanation.

Hindley doesn't seem to notice how panicked I am when I see him. He's even smiling. "When did you get home?" His voice is casual and friendly. His smile doesn't fade at all when I point to the room. He even laughs lightheartedly when my face turns white thinking about all the possibilities that Henry's abandoned bedroom might mean.

"What happened? Tell me what happened to Henry," I demand. Even if it's the worst thing I imagine it to be, I need to know.

"Oh," Hindley says in a relaxed tone. "That's what's worrying you?" He almost sounds relieved about it. Making it seem like it's the silliest thing in the world for me to worry about.

"Where is he?"

"Calm down, he's fine," he says, putting his hand on my shoulder. I shake it off because I know how he works. He always tries to buddy up with me whenever he's done something he knows is going to piss me off.

"Where . . . is . . . he?" I ask, pausing between each word so that Hindley knows to stop playing around.

"In the basement" is the only answer he gives me. It's another part of his game. He'll never say anything more until I ask why. This time I have to ask twice and then a third before he finally gives in. "Because," he says. "That's where his room is from now on."

"Was that his idea?" I ask.

I can tell Hindley wants to say yes. That he's planned on saying yes, but he turns back at the last second. "No, it's mine," he confesses because he enjoys being mean too much not to take credit for it.

"That's not fair! Why would you do that?" I shout, feeling bolder now that I know Henry isn't trying to get away from me. It's all making sense to me now. I should have known it was something like this. I should've figured out that it's Hindley who wants to keep us apart.

"Frances and I want to make this the baby's nursery, like it was before, when you and I were little," he says.

"You mean like it was before Henry!" I yell. I'm sick of him trying to talk around things. All week he's been plotting against Henry and making up some excuse for every decision he's made against him. Telling me he's doing something because of this or that reason instead of just coming out and admitting it's because he hates Henry and that's it.

"Same thing," he says. "Besides, don't you think you're getting a little too old to practically be sharing a room with him?"

"NO! I DON'T!" I yell. "Don't you think you're getting too old to be a jerk all the time?"

Hindley's face splits in a cruel smirk.

"No, I don't," he says as if this whole thing is a joke. "He was never supposed to be part of this family. I'm just fixing things that Dad screwed up." All the hatred he's saved up over all these years flashes against his eyes as he says it.

I always knew he didn't like Henry but I never thought he'd be this jealous. I'd been too wrapped up in the funeral and trying to feel normal again that I didn't see this coming. I never thought that he would take it this far. But it all makes sense now. He's trying to get rid of Henry. It's what he's always wanted.

"You took him out of school, didn't you?" I ask. I'm starting to put the pieces together. "You made him send me that message?" Hindley's smile grows wider as I tell him I won't let him get away with this.

"Unfortunately for Henry, you can't stop me," he says.

"Well, you can't stop me from being with him!" I scream. I don't even look at him as I rush past. I don't want to let him see how my eyes have gotten swollen and blurry. I refuse to let him see that he can get to me. It only makes him worse when he knows.

My legs work without me having to think about it, carrying me down two steps at a time until I get to the first floor. The basement door is open when I reach it. Its damp smell drifts into the laundry room as I go down.

I know this is all my fault. I could've stopped this if I came home right after school. I know I could have. All I would've had to do is stand in the door to Henry's room and keep Hindley from butting in. He'd have cursed at me and screamed about how he was in charge. I'd scream back just as loud, then that would be it. He'd give up the same way he's always given up because he knows he's wrong.

I wait at the bottom of the basement stairs long enough to wipe my eyes. If I want to go in there and tell Henry that everything is going to be fine, I need to act like I believe it. But even if I wait here an hour it won't make a difference. The moment I see Henry slumped over on the bed with his head buried in his hands, I start to cry all over again.

He lifts his head slightly. He peeks at me through his fingers, then he sits up straighter to hide how miserable he feels. His stuff is littered all over the room. Stacks and piles of things that all belong four floors above us are thrown around down here. It's like he's been buried or something. It breaks my heart to see him like this.

"Hi," I say softly. I try to make it sound cheerful but it just comes out like the saddest noise I've ever made. I make my way toward him and sit down next to him on the bed. "Why didn't you tell me?" I ask. "You could've told me this morning. I would've stopped him."

"I know," he says. Then he leans back, raising his eyes to the ceiling like he's searching for some kind of answer that makes sense.

I wait for him to find one, but he never does.

I put my hand on his leg and feel him jump a little at my touch. I fight the feeling to pull away, keeping perfectly still until his breathing goes back to normal. I time my breaths the same as his, in when he does, out too so it's like we're even closer together than just our bodies sitting next to each other.

"This will all blow over," I tell him. "Once the baby is born, Hindley will have other things to worry about. They'll probably just go back to L.A. after that. It'll just be until then."

"Yeah," Henry says but I can tell he doesn't really mean it. I can't blame him. I'm not really sure that I mean it. I'm not sure I'm not just saying it to make us both feel better.

"It'll never work anyway," I say. "He can send you to another school, move you to another room, even another country, but he'll never be able to split us up. I promise." Then I move in closer, bringing my face inches from his so that he can see that I mean it. So he can look in my eyes and know that I'll keep my promise forever because we need each other the same way as the land needs the ocean. That's how the stars mean for us to be. Always looking out for each other.

Henry lowers his head and looks at me. There's nothing in his eyes that says the same thing back. It's almost like he didn't hear me, like I'm already losing him even though he's right here.

"Right? We'll always be together?" I ask him.

It takes a second for the words to settle in. A flash of recognition against the dark center of his eyes.

"Right," he says, so quietly that I almost can't hear him.

FIVE

The shop window is decorated with teddy bears dressed in tie-dyed clothes with corny sayings about long strange trips and other not-so-subtle drug references. Typical for San Francisco, especially on Haight. It's the kind of stuff we're sick to death of. Like people in New York probably hate those I NY shirts. That's why it surprises me when I'm pulled into the trap the way the lights of an amusement park attract little children. "Let's go in here! Please!" I beg, staring with my face pressed to the glass. Everyone else is rolling their eyes and trying to pull me along because not going in those tourist stores is a strict rule. There's nothing cool about those things.

"Jesus, Catherine!" Nelly laughs. "How much of that shit did you smoke?"

"Not too much," I say with a shy smile.

Truth is, it was probably way too much. I've never done it before, though, so I'm not sure. It didn't seem like too much. Edgar and his friends didn't seem concerned that it was. And they all had more. They seemed fine. I mean we only smoked a little.

Maybe that's all it takes, though. I'm not an expert.

Neither is Nelly even if she acts like she is. She's only done it once before and she told me she fell asleep right away. So that doesn't really count.

I never planned on doing it. It just sort of happened. We were hanging out in the park after school and ran into Edgar and some of his friends. They were smoking and invited us to join them. I didn't want to seem like a freak or anything. Besides, everyone in San Fran does it. It's no big deal. And it was nice to fit in without having to think about it.

"We're not going into any store called Never Fade Away," Nelly says. She's firm on that point. Her arms are folded in front of her and her skinny legs are planted in the middle of the sidewalk.

Other people have to step around her but she doesn't seem to notice. Her eyes are so half closed, I wonder if she notices them at all.

"Your eyes . . . they're disappearing," I tell her.

"I'm Korean, remember? I have small eyes," she says sarcastically.

"No, that's not it," I say. I point at them and reach closer until my finger touches her face. "It's like a mystery or something."

She slaps at my hand like swatting a bug, laughing as she does it. "You're out of control!"

"No," Edgar corrects her, "she's just stoned."

I don't know why, but it sounds like the funniest joke ever told. I have to lean against the shop window to keep my balance. Edgar is laughing too. Maybe he's laughing at me but it doesn't matter. It doesn't make me self-conscious at all. It's strange how comfortable I've become around him the last few weeks. We've been hanging out a lot since Henry's permanently grounded. Or acts like it anyway. Hindley says he's not, but Henry never hangs out anymore, so I'm not so sure Hindley's telling me the truth. Either way, though, it means I've been spending more time with Edgar.

I think it kind of bothers Nelly a little. She doesn't say so. But she doesn't have to. It shows in her face every time Edgar's hands touch my arm or my waist or my knee under the lunch table. It's strange. I mean, she pushed me into being with him, then gets all weird now that we're like a thing. I don't know, maybe she feels left out. At least that's how it feels. Like today, she's been on my case ever since I made the suggestion that we go see what Edgar was up to. I don't know why. She was never like this when we hung out with Henry. But I guess that was different. I don't think she ever thought of me and Henry the same way.

"Do we have to stand here all day?" she asks.

I take another peek in the window, watching how the shadows dance in the crystal figurines each time a car passes between them and the sun. Fairy statues with jewelry eyes that blink awake when the light strikes them. Their sparkling glass like a time machine that slows everything down and I forget that I'm holding everyone up. "Um, no. We can go," I say.

Nelly rolls her eyes. "Really, Catherine, you're such a scatterbrain sometimes." She starts to walk away and I watch the way her knees bend beneath her skirt. She has such a perfect runway walk. It makes everyone want to watch her as she passes through the swelling Friday afternoon crowd of kids killing time and tourists snapping pictures.

"You know, Cat, we can go in there if you really want to," Edgar says.

I smile whenever he calls me that. Cat. He made it up a few days ago when we were on the lawn before school. I climbed up to the first branch of the willow tree and draped my legs over the side. Edgar said I climbed like a cat.

Cat.

Catherine.

It just kind of stuck. It's a little silly, but it's still new enough that it makes me smile. Maybe it always will.

"That's okay. I don't really want to go in," I tell him. "It was just the way the glass glittered that I liked."

When we start to walk, it almost feels like the morning fog has stayed inside me even though the sky is clear and golden. I let Edgar take my hand and lead me through the people coming toward us in the other direction. Coming at us like waves that break apart before our eyes. Splitting up and spreading out only to come back together again after we trade our place on the sidewalk with theirs. We weave through the crowd but it never lets up. It's like life is stuck in slow motion. Only the constant tapping of my shoes seems to move forward at the right speed. The rest of the city moves in a strange rhythm that makes me breathe faster. Makes me want to hold on to him tighter to help me walk straighter.

Nelly would say that's what's supposed to happen if I shared any of my feelings with her. If I told her that I feel every drop of blood as it swims through my veins. She'd say I was being weird if I said it almost tickles, that it feels like the way the wind feels blowing against my bare skin after skinny-dipping in the ocean.

84

If I told Edgar, he would probably smile. But I don't know if he'd understand. He always smiles at the strange things I say. But not like he gets it, just like he thinks it's interesting that I'm so different. That I'm rare and that makes me more valuable.

Henry would know exactly what I mean. If I told Henry that every time I breathe, the air tastes like sunshine, he'd understand. If I told him how the crowded sidewalks make me just the right amount of dizzy that it feels a little like falling and that falling feels a little like flying, then he'd know what that means too. I wouldn't even have to say it aloud. He'd know just by the way my hand would tremble in his. Or he used to anyway.

I miss that.

I miss everything about him.

Nothing has really blown over like I thought it would. Hindley treats him like a servant and now it's almost like Henry is embarrassed to be around me. It's like he wants to forget about anything that reminds him how everything used to be. Ever since he moved into the basement, it's like he just wants to vanish from the face of the earth. Even when I am with him, it's like he isn't there. I can't get more than a few words out of him at a time. Like he's trying to get rid of me as soon as possible.

I know he's just feeling sorry for himself, but it's not good for him to sulk the way he does. I've told him acting that way only encourages Hindley to be worse. If that's even possible! He's been so terrible already.

"It sucks and it's not fair," I told Henry. "But you can't let it get to you. You can't stop hanging out with your friends because of it. It's like you're helping him or something."

Henry nodded but he hasn't done anything to change it.

Nelly says I should put it out of my mind. "You can't stop living your life just because Henry's decided to check out." She's probably right. I shouldn't worry so much. He'll snap out of it. I know he will. But I can't help it. Things just pop into my head all the time and he's the only one I want to tell them to.

I can't just sit around and watch Henry be miserable. If he keeps pushing me away, I'll need to push back harder. I've made up my mind about it when we reach the next DON'T WALK sign. "I know," I say, saying it like suddenly answering a question that no one asked.

Edgar raises his eyebrows and looks at me. He gets so curious about what I'm going to say whenever something bursts out of me like that. It makes me nervous to get so much of his attention, so I lower my eyes and watch the way my foot dangles over the edge of the curb as a paper cup rolls along the gutter.

Nelly gives me the look again that says I'm flaking.

But I know what I'm doing. It's what I have to do.

"Let's go back to my place," I say, twisting a little with my hips, swinging my foot back and forth, making it sound like there's no other reason except that it's something to do. "We can head down to the beach and wait for the stars to come out."

"Sounds fine to me," Edgar says.

"Sounds boring to me," Nelly says.

Everything gets tense and I turn away from her. I fold my arms and stare off in the direction of the taller buildings downtown. Edgar senses it. His hand comes to rest on my shoulder. A sudden soft touch that makes me shiver.

"I think we should," he says.

"Really?" I ask.

"Sure, why not?"

Nelly shakes her head. "Fine," she says. "Whatever."

I can tell she's mad by the way she falls behind us. I know she wants to stay and hang around until the electric signs switch on and the city comes alive with voices scattered up and down every popular street. Anything but sit around. And that's why she comes up behind me and whispers in my ear, "Is Henry going to be home? What's he going to do when he sees Edgar?" trying to change my mind.

She knows I've been careful to keep them from seeing each other. Keeping most of my time with Edgar a secret because I know Henry would get angry. Or he would have before. I'm not so sure anymore. I mean, he's the one pulling away, so maybe that means he doesn't care so much. Or maybe it's just me who doesn't care so much anymore because keeping them apart isn't as important as getting Henry to snap out of this mood he's been in.

"So what if he is?" I say to her. "What's wrong with wanting him to hang out with us?"

"It's cool with me," Edgar says. "I don't mind if Henry hangs out with us. You spend enough time with Isabelle that I'm surprised they haven't made you a saint yet." Then he nods in the direction we need to walk, making sure I know it's okay. He really doesn't mind.

"Thanks," I whisper back at him.

Nelly rolls her eyes and shrugs, letting me know she thinks I'm making a mistake but that it's my mistake to make and none of her business. Lately, it's like I can't do anything right with her.

The mood of the whole afternoon changes during the silent walk up to Fulton Street to catch the bus. Each of us has slipped away into our own thoughts. We drift apart at the bus stop. Nelly looks at flyers posted on the side of a building advertising which concerts are coming up, which movies are coming out, and what clothes we should buy. Edgar studies the cars that drive by. There's a few feet between us. Enough so that he doesn't feel comfortable telling me which car is which like he usually does. His eyes usually get big and excited as he tells me how many miles per hour a certain car can go, how rare a particular model might be, or which cars he might want once he's got his driver's license. He lights up when he talks about those things. I wish he would talk about them now even though I could really care less about cars. It would just bring us all back if one of us started talking.

I see him twitch.

His mouth makes the start of a word but he holds it in. He retreats and I guess that's what they call "coming down." We all are. Each of us sinking into ourselves as the bus pulls up. We all board in silence and take our seats.

I keep my face pressed against the window as we drive past the park. The people look like bright polka dots against the trees. They run together into shapes and lines when the bus moves faster and fall to individual pieces when the bus stops again.

"Pretty cool, huh?" Nelly whispers from the seat in front of me. She's smiling, staring out the window at the same scene I am.

I smile back at her. "Yeah," I say and start to feel better.

It's funny how that happens. How I can think I'm drifting so far away but then I find out that the people I'm with are really drifting to the same place. It's like that with Nelly most of the *time. It's always been like that with Henry too. So there's still a chance we can drift back together.*

✢ ✢

I don't see them coming in time. It's too late to turn around, they've already spotted me .. sprayed a target on me with their eyes .. zeroed in. If I turn around, they'll just follow me .. their footsteps will echo mine through the abandoned hall and that'll only make it worse because then they'll know I'm scared of them. I've been playing this elaborate game of hide-and-seek at school for weeks .. ducking down corridors .. dipping into classrooms, bathrooms, and gyms .. anything to keep from being found. I've avoided most fights that way .. got off with just a few scuffles but this time, I'm too slow. There's nothing left for me to do but put my head down and walk into their trap.

Vick has them ready.

He's had his whole crew ready since the first day I got to Bayside. They've been harassing me behind my back for the most part .. warning anybody from siding with me .. letting the whole school know I'm marked for an ass kicking because he never liked the look of me. He's ready to make good on those promises now.

I peek up and see him tap two of his henchmen on the shoulder and jerk his head in my direction. One kid moves to his right side .. the other moves to his left .. Vick stays a few inches in front of them both. Assault formation .. uniforms of low-hanging jeans and sleeveless T-shirts showing off homemade tattoos burned on their arms with ballpoint pens. Identical expressions on their faces.. crooked smiles telling strangers not to mess with them.

—Hey! Hey! Here he comes— Vick says like a game show host announcing the next contestant as I approach.. mock applause and one eye held open wider than the other. —Look at him strutting. Thinks he's the Prince of Downtown— The other two kids laugh as Vick spits on the floor.. showing his teeth like an angry dog when he looks back at me. —Rich trash! What the hell you doing here, boy?—

I keep my mouth shut.

He can talk all the shit he wants just as long he leaves after he's said what he needs to say.

The bigger kid starts tapping his fist against a locker.. a steady bang that gets faster.. the feel of it like an earthquake when the row of lockers rattles. Vick steps up to me.. his feet in sync with the fist tapping against metal. I pull at the strap of my backpack.. shift my weight from one leg to the other and lift my head up.. stare him down, eye to eye. Vick isn't any bigger than me. He can't take me and that's the only reason they've waited this long to lay into me like they've wanted to.. waited until it was uneven.. three against one and no one around to put an end to it before they've finished.

—Look.. I got no problem with you— I say. I hold my hands out in front of me and try to wave him off with a peace warning.

Vick takes his hands out of his pockets.. his fingers folding into fists as he looks me up and down. —That's too bad, see? 'Cause we got problems with you, Harry—

—Henry— I tell him.

—Don't matter whatever you're called— he barks back.
—Never heard of no Puerto Rican with either name—

—I'm not Puerto Rican— I tell him.

—What are you trying to say? Something wrong with
being Puerto Rican?— getting all defensive.. saying he's
Puerto Rican.. so are the two boys at his back. It's an old
playground game.. trying to pick a fight by twisting my
words around.. making up a reason to fight just to say he
had a reason.

—I didn't say that—

—Yeah, well, what did you say?— He takes a step closer..
a taste for violence in the way he pushes the words off his
tongue.. quick slashing words like the three lines shaved
into his eyebrows.

—I didn't say anything— I mumble.. shaking my head
at how pointless all of this is. Like it proves anything to anyone if we stand here and growl at each other or if he and his
friends gang up on me. I've had enough of him.. of this
place.. of everything and I just want to be left alone.

I step around him and start walking.

Vick lowers his shoulder into my chest.. an impact like
cement hitting bone and I feel air escape my lungs in a hurried gasp. I stumble when his sneakers tangle up with my legs
and he shoves me.. pushing me to the floor so that my head
strikes against the lockers. —What you got to say now, rich
boy?— spitting his words at me as my eyes water from the
pain of trying to catch my breath.

I've got nothing to say.. no air to say it with.. and no

91

way of stopping all three of them when they crowd around me like angry birds over another one who's left for dead. All I can do is cover my face and take a few kicks to my side. A burning sharp pain each time they strike.. raining blows on me for a minute and then it's all over.

Vick calls off his pets.

They stand still and grin over their prey.

—Just because you live up in the Heights, you still ain't nothing. You wouldn't be down here in Bayside if you was, re-member that— Vick warns.. laughing as he bends down closer.. stealing the baseball cap off my head to make sure his message sinks in before tossing it down the hall. I watch it slide past one classroom after another as they take off after it.. keeping it going like kids kicking stones along the street.. going and going until they disappear at the end of the hall.

A teacher sticks her head out of the classroom door as I slowly get to my feet. —What's going on out here? You can't be here— she says.. letting me know that I'm a prob-lem.. a distraction.. that I need to leave and that she doesn't care what went on before or what goes on after she returns to her safe classroom, just as long as I'm gone by the time she looks out again.

Fine with me.

This whole building can go to hell for all I care! Everyone in it can rot and I wouldn't give a shit! Vick was right about one thing.. the people in this place really are nothing.. not worth arguing with and not worth fighting.

Not me, though.

I'm not like them and I won't ever be like them.

Hindley can send me to the worst school in the city.. give me all the lousy chores in the world.. treat me no better than a dog, but I won't ever be like Vick. I made a promise. I swore to Catherine that I wouldn't let all of this get to me.

It gets harder each day to keep that promise.

Hindley's doing everything he can to drive us apart. He watches me every second he's home. I need to be careful about even talking to her. I have cut every conversation with her short because I can feel him looking over my shoulder.. just waiting to catch us. It's killing me. Not being able to hang out with her.. to tell her all the things that I'm thinking about. Some days go by and I don't even get to hear the sound of her voice.

I only need to hold out a little longer, though.. just long enough to get him to tear up those papers. I got to stay on my best behavior until then.. stay out of trouble. It's working so far.. I feel like he's letting up a bit.. getting bored now he sees it hasn't worked out the way he thought. I haven't been giving him shit, he hasn't been getting calls home from the school, and Catherine isn't giving up on me. It must be so boring for him.

I catch my reflection in the glass part of the door as I head out of school. A few scrapes but nothing too bad. Most of the pain is hidden. Nothing the sun's glare won't cure as I get on the bus and head home. It takes an hour or so to get back. I use the time to clear my head.. watch the city pass by like a moving painting until it lulls me to sleep. And when I open my eyes again, the Heights is right where I left it.. waiting for me to step into the cool shade of the houses.

Shadows cover the sidewalk with the color of rain that hasn't fallen yet..the soft shade cast by a fog that won't settle on the ground until the sun dies for the day and the clouds collapse trying to follow it to the other side of the world. Our house stands taller than the shadows can reach..still bleached by the shine of the California sun that sometimes lets people make believe that our city is carved from gold instead of bricks and stone and cement rusting in the salty air that touches the tip of my tongue every time I breathe.

I can see our house from the end of the block. I stare at the top floor as my sneakers kick gravel stones across the sidewalk. It used to always feel like Heaven on the top floor..always so safe and warm that it used to seem as permanent as the weather..never changing, the way the seasons never change here. Catherine and I used to say our lives were going to be like that..never changing..because our fate was written to be perfect forever.

Now I notice how the shade seems to reach the house easier than it ever did before..makes the white paint appear damp..makes the whole place seem cold. The shadows are heavier and it doesn't resemble the sun so much anymore..more like a star that is going dim.

But it'll return to normal soon.

I'll make sure of it.

A faint coughing distracts me and I glance over to see Isabelle sitting on her porch as I pass..swinging her legs slowly..lifting them higher as I get closer so that the sun erases the shadows on her thighs..a flash of her underwear on purpose before she brings her knees closer together again.

—Hi— she says .. her short black curls dangling against her cheek .. dark strands that look like clouds passing in front of a full moon before she tosses them out of the way with a flick of her wrist.

I turn away from her .. a stabbing pain shoots through my side where Vick's knee struck. I clutch at it and shake it off .. cursing Isabelle quietly under my breath as I let the pain seep out with a sigh .. blaming her for making me relive it all over again.

She laughs when I continue walking.

She always finds it amusing when I try to avoid her .. like a game where she makes up all the rules .. a game I'm not even playing but that only makes her more determined to come after me because that's the way she is .. always wanting attention and it doesn't even matter what kind of attention it is.

She hops down and takes up after me like a stray .. the skipping sound of her sandals on the sidewalk closing the distance until she's right beside me. —Hey, don't you want to talk to me?— she asks with a pout in her voice.

I've never wanted to talk to her in my life .. even less now than ever before, so I don't answer .. counting down the spaces in the sidewalk between the Lintons' house and ours. She's faster, though .. fast enough to get in front of me and block the way .. crossing her arms .. putting on like I've hurt her feelings and asking me why I don't like her.

—Just get away from me— making my voice sound like a threat .. looking at her through the top of my eyes like a cornered animal close to snapping, but she doesn't flinch .. lets a playful smile come to her lips.

—You should be nicer to me, Henry— she says. She turns her body slowly at her hips.. twisting carefully so that I can see the shape of her bra stretching against the thin tank top.. tucking her bottom lip under her clean white teeth and smiling wider.. blinking her blue eyes at the sun until I look away.

I try to step around her but she reaches out.. her small fingers wrapping weakly around my elbow before I shake them off.

—You know, we're practically going to be relatives soon— she says.. her mouth closer to my ear as she says it like it's a secret.. her hand moving quickly back to my arm.. sliding her palm in small circles over my skin.

I pull away too fast and suffer another sharp pain beneath my ribs.. making me growl at her in a voice angrier than before. —What are you talking about?—

Isabelle pulls away and wrinkles her forehead. —Catherine and Edgar.. what, are you blind or something?—

I shake my head because she's got it all wrong.

She doesn't know anything about anything.

—It's true— Isabelle whines. —They're always together now— she says with a show of disgust on her face. —I wish they'd just get it over with and make out already—

The thought of Catherine being that close to Edgar makes my heart race.. picturing his mouth covering hers.. his hands crawling beneath her clothes like hungry ghosts. Thinking about it makes my muscles tense up.

—Is she over there now?— I ask.

Isabelle smiles and shakes her head.

—No— she says. —My brother ditched me today to hang out with your sister somewhere—

—Where?— I ask.

Isabelle shrugs her shoulders.

—Not here— she says. —But that doesn't mean you can't come over—

I sigh and start to walk away again. I've had enough of her. It's probably all bullshit anyway.. everything she's said. Catherine would never be interested in that idiot.

Isabelle calls me back but I don't listen.

—Henry!— she shouts again, but I wave her off without looking.. step onto the porch and have my hand on the door when she says that she sees them. —They're coming now.. at the end of the block—

I turn my head to where she's pointing. Three figures are walking into the glare of the sun. Catherine's in the middle, waving at me before breaking free and hurrying ahead.. her hair bouncing against her shoulders each time her sneakers make contact with the ground.. her arms spread out to her sides the way a bird would and watching her only makes me miss her more.

She's out of breath as she steps onto the porch. —I was hoping you'd be here— she says, grabbing hold of one of the posts and leaning back.. her body hovering over the edge of the steps with her back arched like a rainbow. Then she smiles.. the kind of smile she saves just for me.. the one that makes her freckles disappear and it's like the last few days of silence between us have never happened.. like time is standing still long enough for us to remember how things were before Mr. Earnshaw died . . before Hindley and Frances ruined our lives.

But time can't stop forever no matter how much I want it to. It creaks forward again, bringing Nelly and Edgar with it.

They stand on the lawn with blank smiles painted on their faces . . squinting to keep the sun out of their eyes. The smell hits me then . . one every kid in the Bay area knows. They've all been getting high and Edgar keeps covering his mouth . . mumbling things that make Nelly laugh and I can feel tension building behind my eyes . . an angry pain that reminds me just how much I hate him. I've got to get Catherine to stop hanging out with him. She'd never have done that on her own. She's nothing like him . . like his friends. She's better . . like the brightest star in the sky . . more beautiful than the others that only exist to distract attention away from her.

—We're going to the beach . . you want to come with us?— she asks . . swaying side to side . . dangling over the lawn like it's a dangerous thing to do even though it's only two feet below because she's nervous I'll turn her down the way I've turned down all her invitations lately. —We thought it'd be fun—

—Sounds like it— I say . . but I'm lying. It only sounds like fun as long it's just me and her . . as long as no one else comes with us.

—Then you're going to come with us?— Catherine asks . . an excited pitch in her voice that will make it harder for me to reject her.

—I . . I can't— I have to force the words out because every part of me wants to say —yes— wants to ignore all of Hindley's threats and see what happens. But then I look at her..how perfect she is even when she looks sad..even when her eyes tell me she's upset with me for letting her down. I hate seeing her this way but I don't have a choice..either see her like this or not at all.

Nelly tugs at the bottom of Catherine's shirt so that she'll let go and settle back on the lawn with them. Then Nelly turns to me..shaking her head and making her eyes like arrows. —What's up with you anyway?—

—Nothing— I lie. —I just..I have stuff I got to do—

—If you do it later, I'll help you— Catherine says.

—Yeah, come on, man! Hang with us for a little bit— Edgar says.

I narrow my eyes and stare at him..study the lazy smile on his face..the way his head moves in the wind like a balloon..like something inflated that I could burst with one swing.

—I can't— telling it to Catherine and only her.

Her smile wilts completely as she sinks away. Edgar takes his hands from his pockets and touches her arm..slides his palm from her elbow to her wrist..stealing the warm sunlight that rests on her skin like a halo..so casual..like it's something he's used to doing and I don't understand why she's not horrified by the feel of his fingerprints as they trace the shape of her bones.

His eyes are on her too..staring at the start of a smile on her lips..a faraway look in her eyes as she looks back at him. And I don't know if I step off the porch because of the way his hand is touching her or because of the way Catherine is smiling at him in a way that tells me they share a private world the way only she and I are supposed to.

It doesn't matter what the reason is once I go at him. It's too late to stop after that.. once my fist cracks against his jaw.. once he falls to the ground.. reasons don't matter much after that. I just keep going. My hands lock onto Edgar's shoulders.. lifting him up and slamming his head down to the grass.. a dull sound like boots stomping through mud.. repeating it over and over.. caught in a loop that I can't stop.. that I don't want to stop.

Catherine starts screaming then.. begging me to let him go.. wanting it to end and I hear her but I don't listen. All I can think about is how she smiled at him and how it means he's stealing her from me.. swooping in like some vulture the second I step out of the picture.. snatching her away from me as soon as I was defenseless. There's a price to pay for that. Thinking he can take, take, take just like all of the spoiled assholes on this block. Well, he can't take her.. and I'll keep pounding on him until I'm sure he's learned.

—Henry? Stop!— she yells.. tries to pull me off because she doesn't understand yet that I'm doing this for us. She keeps repeating my name.. each time making it sound farther away.. each time more like the name of a stranger than someone she's promised to spend the rest of her life with and that only makes me more driven to punish Edgar.

It's Hindley who finally makes me stop. His arms twisting mine behind my back.. cursing me as I struggle to get away.. trying to fight back as he drags me into the house because everything I've held in over the last several weeks has finally broken at the seams.

I'm like an animal in his grasp..I feel it in my limbs..in the way my blood is running through my veins like liquid metal. And I only stop trying to wrestle free when I see Catherine's eyes go dim as she looks at me..seeing what I see in the kids that attacked me in the hallway..seeing me as someone she's afraid of and that's when I surrender.

I don't even bother to put my hands up to protect my face when Hindley strikes me..not the first punch or the second. I let him hit me as many times as he likes because if I can make the light in her eyes fade..if I can make something so beautiful disappear even for a second..then maybe I really am a monster. Maybe she does need to be kept away from me.

When Hindley pushes me down the basement steps and locks the door, I don't try to get up. I don't scream for him to let me out. I curl up in a ball and stay on the floor where I am, aware that I've messed everything up.

SIX

*L*ately it's like our home is dying.
  Or sick at least.

There are symptoms of it everywhere. Signs of it in the silent looks that pass between me and Henry. The way everything remains unspoken.

We don't talk about what happened but it's all we think about. I think about it so much that it suffocates me. I can't stop thinking it's my fault. That maybe I should have known Henry would react like that. That I should have been more careful. But thinking about it doesn't change any of it. I can't take it back. I can't make it so it never happened.

It shouldn't bother me so much. It's not like it's the first time Henry's freaked out like that. But he's never done it without a reason before and never quite this bad.

The look in his eyes is the thing that haunts me. It was too clear to forget. Almost like he was erased for a second. All the parts of him that I've always known and relied on got evaporated. Burned away in anger. No matter how hard I try, I can't push it out of my mind. That image of him is everywhere, even in my room, hiding behind all the things that remind me of him. That memory is like a disease that can't be cured right away. It's all around me and if I stay in this house another minute, I'm afraid I'll be permanently infected.

"I'm sorry, I have to get out of here," I tell Nelly.

"Why? I thought we were going to watch a movie," Nelly says, suddenly sitting up on my bed.

"I know," saying it like an apology, "but I can't. Not right now."

Nelly's instantly upset. She's trying to hide it. She's trying to be patient with me because of everything that's going on, but still it shows. The way her arms fall into her lap shows it. The way her eyes shrink and turn their attention to the windows. The way her breath is blown out so strong that it causes her bangs to flutter before settling back against her forehead.

"I promise we'll hang out tomorrow," I tell her, knowing that I probably don't mean it. I'll feel the same way tomorrow. The same as I felt this way yesterday. "I need some fresh air. I need to get out of this room."

"Fine," Nelly says. "Where do you want to go?"

I bring my hand up to my mouth and start to bite my nails.

Nelly shakes her head and sighs again because she knows what it means when I press my fingers against my face and turn my head away from her. "You don't want me to come with you, do you?"

"It's not that," I say. "I just don't want anyone around. I don't want to have to think."

"Does that include Edgar?" she snaps.

I don't have to say anything, she already knows the answer. She knows I'm going to see him just by glancing at me. Just by the guilty way I lower my eyes to watch the way my shoelaces dangle carefully above the floor.

I start to explain that being with him isn't the same but she doesn't let me. She waves away my words as she springs up from the side of the bed. "Just forget it, Cathy!" she shouts. "I get it. Okay? It's not like you're the first person I ever met who ditches their friends for some new boyfriend."

"It isn't like that," I argue.

"It's exactly like that," she says and I'm not sure why she's so against him. I think she feels like I'm picking him over her. I'm not. It's just that when I'm with him, it's easier to forget about how crazy everything here has become. He doesn't ask about any of it. Doesn't force me to talk about it to death or make me feel guilty about anything. And maybe it's like she said earlier, maybe it's because he doesn't really care. Maybe that's okay and maybe it isn't. All I know is that it works for right now.

He makes me feel better.

"Why are you being like this?" I ask, trying to keep her from storming off in a bad mood. Begging almost. Because I already have one best friend not speaking to me that I don't think I could handle another.

She must hear it in my voice because her face softens as she opens the door. "Forget it," she says, shaking her words away with a toss of her head. "Really, it's fine," trying her best to make it sound like she didn't mean any of it.

"I swear, we'll do it tomorrow," I promise.

"Yeah, all right."

She leaves my room as she says it, not even bothering to turn around. I wait for her to disappear before I get up and leave. I wish it hadn't made her mad but I had no choice. I have to get out of here.

⊱ ⊰

—Is it just me or is Catherine no fun anymore?— Nelly blurts out exactly one minute after walking in on me without knocking.. without a word of warning about what she came here to talk about.. just out and says it.. throwing her arms up and falling back in the chair that sits in the corner of the basement.

I stare at her but I don't answer.

I've barely even seen Catherine since that day on the porch almost two weeks ago. Since before then, really.. but now it's different. Now I don't even have to force myself to avoid her because she avoids me. That's when she's home.. she tries not to be as much as possible. Staying out just to stay away. And maybe that's what Nelly means.. maybe it's not just me she's avoiding.

—It's not like I'd know— I mumble.

—Yeah, I guess you're right. You haven't exactly been on her favorite persons list— Nelly says.. trying to take my side but I wish she wouldn't because hearing it from her only makes me feel worse.

—So, what, you came here to cheer me up, then?— I say sarcastically.

—Hey, don't take it so hard— she says. —It's not like she's dying to spend time with me either—

106

—What's that supposed to mean?—

Nelly gives a fake laugh..the kind of laugh she gives when she's mad. —It means she just ditched me to go see Edgar— fluttering her eyes when she says his name the way little kids do when they tease someone about being in love.

—She did?— not able to hide the surprise in my voice because I didn't know it had come to that..that Catherine was feeling that way about him..that she actually wanted to spend time with him.

—For like the thousandth time, where have you been?— she says before she remembers where we are..remembers exactly where I've been. She quickly squeaks out a —sorry— and bites her lip.

—Does she like him or something?— I ask.

Nelly shrugs. —Sure. I think so—

I feel my heart drop..my mouth dry up like dust filling my throat. —Why?— is all I can get out before my eyes start to catch fire thinking about them together.

Nelly hasn't noticed..too busy nosing through my things..saying —Beats me— as she shuffles through some notebooks. —Personally, I don't think they're right for each other. I thought maybe they could be..but now I don't know. She's just not the same around him..not like when the three of us used to hang. That was fun. Too bad, huh?—

I'm not really listening to her. I keep going over it in my head..trying to figure what Catherine could see in him.. wondering if I somehow drove her to him..if I made her feel sorry enough for him that she actually felt something. —I wish I'd really hurt him— I whisper under my breath.

—What?—

—Nothing— I growl —Just I can't believe she's with that dick!—

The words slither off my tongue like a dangerous poison and Nelly's not dumb. She sees it . . the wheels inside her head start spinning . . start figuring out what I've just let slip.

—Wait— she says slowly . . making her eyes into small slits as she examines my expression. —You like her . . you do, don't you?— I grind my teeth . . breathe through my nose and she says that's all the response she needs. —I can tell these things— she says . . saying she can't believe she never figured it out before.

She wants to know everything . . how it happened . . for how long . . why I never said anything . . all the same stupid questions she'd ask about any crush any of her friends had. As if this was the same thing?

Me and Catherine are different.

Me and Catherine are forever.

I can't believe she would turn her back on that . . not for a piece of shit snob like Edgar Linton! Thinking about it makes me nauseous . . talking about it makes me feel even worse. But Nelly's not going to stop . . and not answering her is only going to make her ask again and again until I can't bear it. She keeps saying she can help me . . that she wants to help me.

But what can she really do?

She can't make time go backward . . she can't change things that already happened . . and I'm beginning to think that's the only way things could get back to the way they were.

—I'm going to help you whether you want me to or not, Henry!— Nelly says . . trying to be cheerful and hopeful and however else she can be that might make me smile but I'd rather she just left me alone.

Loneliness is the only really helpful thing she can give me.

⊱ ⊰

The ships are hidden behind the fog. I hear them moaning like whales in the distance. The air heavy with the drone of their horns as we walk along the beach. The fog is so dense, it's impossible to tell where the sky ends and the water begins. The gulls appear out of nowhere like a mystery, swooping down onto the waves and beating the water off their wings violently. Their angry shouts drowned out by the hum of the ocean, churning like a giant storm somewhere just out of sight.

When the weather is like this, I pretend that we're ghosts. There's no future that we can see besides the mist in front of us. No past either because my footprints disappear from the sand the moment I step away. It's almost like we don't exist anywhere except right here, right now.

It used to scare me when I was little. The fog would get so thick that I thought it would never lift. I thought it was the world going blind. That every pretty color was dying.

My dad used to tell me that the fog froze time. He said anything that happened on a day like this would be like a dream. A good dream or a bad one was up to me, but that he always believed in good dreams. But I always believed in bad dreams. Picturing scary creatures coming out of the ocean or imagining the sidewalk ending just a few feet ahead of me where I'd fall and there wasn't any end to the falling.

Henry always wanted me to go for walks on days like this. I'd shake my head and cover my ears so I couldn't hear him begging me. "Come on, Catherine! It'll be fun, I swear!" Eventually he'd wear me down, pull my hands away from my ears, and drag me onto the porch. I would stay there. My hands clutching the posts as he walked into the fog. I'd watch him walk slowly, and he'd stop every two steps to ask if I could still see him.

I remember how my heart would beat so fast the second he vanished. "Come back!" I'd shout and he would laugh, the sound letting me know exactly how far he'd gone.

After a while, it didn't scare me so much. It was fun to guess how far he could get before disappearing. We'd play a game of charades with our voices. He'd make noises and ask me to guess what he was pretending to be. Then I started taking turns too. Short trips off the porch and it was so strange being in the middle of nothing. It was like the entire city was empty.

The first couple of times I made Henry come with me. It was too lonely disappearing all by myself. I liked it when he was with me, though. Now I'm used to it, of course. I'm not afraid like I was when we were little kids. But I still like it better when someone is with me. It's just better turning into a ghost with someone else by your side.

"Crazy, huh?" Edgar says.

"Hmmm?" I mumble, tucking my hair behind my ears as I look over at him. The breeze returns then, carrying a faint mist off the ocean that touches my face and I have the sleepy feeling of having just woken from a nap.

"The fog," he says. "It's something else, right?" Tilting his head to look at the sky, so heavy with clouds that it sits all around us.

I switch the sneakers from my left hand to carry them in my right. Check to make sure my socks are still stuffed safely inside. Then I put my free hand into his. "It's nice," I say, talking about the way he holds my hand as much as I'm talking about the weather.

"Yeah," he says, turning toward me to smile and he's just close enough for me to be able to see him. I smile back and let my eyes linger on his face for a second before we start walking again.

It's been almost two weeks, but if I let my eyes go out of focus I can still make out the bruise around his eye where Henry attacked him. The way the sun filters through the fog makes it more visible almost. Brings out the painful shade of blue hiding under the skin above his cheekbone.

He catches me staring and puts his other hand up to his face. His fingers touching the bruise for a split second before he pulls his arm away. "It's gone, really," he says. "You can stop fussing about it. It's not a big deal."

It's not true.

The way Henry went after him was a big deal. Henry's temper showed so suddenly and spread so swiftly that it was like the air around him caught on fire. Red sparks turning his dark eyes into flames. Swirling around him like gasoline rainbows in the wind. When he pinned Edgar to the ground, it was like he was trying to burn him alive.

He was like the monsters I dreamed would climb out of the ocean.

I hate thinking of him that way. That's not Henry.

I shut my eyes. Press them closed so tight that I can only see bright purple rings that block out the memory, letting it get burned away by the bright outlines.

"How is he anyway?" Edgar asks.

"Henry?" I'm surprised he cares. I wouldn't blame him for not caring. Henry's been nothing but terrible to him since we've been kids. "I didn't think you'd want to know," I say.

Edgar sort of shrugs. "Your brother kind of freaked out on him, huh?"

"Yeah. He did." I look down as I say it. Watch my bare feet slide into the sand so that I don't have to remember the wild look in Hindley's eyes that wasn't any different than the one in Henry's. Both of them so full of hate for each other that they might just ruin everything around them.

"That must suck," he says.

"What?"

"Just the fighting all the time," Edgar says. "I mean, you'd think they'd try to get along. It's hard enough about your dad and it seems like they're just making things worse."

"You have no idea," I say. "It's been awful. All the shouting and screaming. Hindley acts like such a tyrant. They go at it all the time. It's like Henry doesn't see that it only makes Hindley that much harder on him."

"Have you told him that?"

I shake my head. "No, he wouldn't listen to me anyway," I say. "He won't even talk to me anymore."

I'm not exaggerating either.

I stopped going to his room after a few days of him not answering when I knocked. He wouldn't even tell me to go away or anything. He just ignored me. And it's not like I want to give up on him, but I just don't know what to do anymore.

I know it can't ever be like before. Maybe it never even should've been like that. But it doesn't have to be like this either. I don't want us to be strangers in the same house. We're too close to end up like that. But I'm starting to think he wants to give up on us ever being close again.

"I feel like maybe it's my fault a little," Edgar says, letting his fingers slip away from mine.

It's sweet how much he worries about me. That he actually worries about me and Henry despite everything that's happened. It's the kind of thing I should've told Nelly about to make her understand. But it's also the kind of thing that's too hard to explain. A feeling that doesn't really work with words. The kind that makes it so easy to be with him.

I move closer to him. Let my arms slide around his waist until my hands lock behind his back. I rest my cheek against his chest, listening as his heartbeat grows quicker. This is what I should have told her too. About how when I'm pressed up this close to him, everything feels like it will always be okay for as long as he holds me.

The fog starts to lift off the surface of the water and I can see the glimmer of sunbeams on the waves like the tips of electric fish coming up for air. Edgar's hands feel the same way on my shoulders. Moving back and forth like the comfortable rhythm of the water. Moving up from my shoulders and under my hair and I can feel his touch on the back of my neck when I look up at him.

His eyes are the last thing I see before we kiss.

They fade into the color of the clearing sky and it's like they've become part of me when our mouths meet. Like he becomes part *of me when we breathe together. The sky does too. The ocean. The sand. Even the sun that is suddenly shining through and tickling my arms. And that's what makes it different from the private world Henry and I used to share. It doesn't feel the same when I'm kissing Edgar, because with us, it doesn't feel like we're leaving the rest of the world behind. It feels like we're part of it. Like everything in it is part of us.*

When I open my eyes again, things feel different.

The fog has gone.

The city feels alive in the distance. The beach feels alive with people. The birds flying in flocks, making shadow trails that bend over tiny hills in the sand so that it even seems to be breathing along with me. I rest my head on his shoulder and watch.

"I really like you," Edgar says.

"Me too," I say.

A trace of me still on his lips.

⚘⚘

The fog keeps any daylight from creeping into the small windows . . makes the room even drearier than normal . . sealing me off from the world like a tomb. At least it feels like . . feels like I might as well be dead already with how things are going lately.

Nelly hasn't let up . . still going at it the same as when she started.

—Well, you have to do something— she says . . leafing through the pile of drawings on my desk . . just sketches of birds that I've done for Catherine the last few weeks . . stupid ones I did in class to take my mind off of being there. I'd never give them to her. I don't care if Nelly thinks she'd like them. Because I know that Catherine would only pretend to like them. I doubt she even remembers how the birds were the last good secret we shared.

Lately it seems like she's forgetting all about me.

—What's the point?— I say. —You said it yourself, all she cares about is Edgar— Catherine's always said that Capricorns are always climbing.. charging ahead while fish like me are left behind trying to tread water. I might as well give up and drown already.

Nelly sighs.. drops the drawings back into the pile on the desk.. throwing them into just enough of a mess to let me know she's annoyed.

—That's why you need to do something!— she says.

I roll over on the bed.

I've had enough of her lecturing me.

She's been at it all afternoon.. going over one elaborate scheme after the other.. each time promising me that her plan —*will win Catherine over*— I can't get her to shut up about her latest and greatest plan.. me surprising Catherine with those stupid sketches and writing some crappy emo poem to go with them. She swears Catherine will be swept off her feet. The whole thing is dumb, though. I shouldn't even have to win her over. We're just supposed to be together.. she's supposed to know that the same way I do.

—If you just stay here feeling sorry for yourself, then she's going to end up with Edgar— Nelly says. —You'll have no one to blame but yourself— tossing her head back and saying it to me like she's my parent or something.

—I have plenty of people I can blame— I sneer.

I blame Hindley for starters..bossing me around like I'm a maid or something and blackmailing me to stay away from her. He's been driving us apart from the second he showed up here..like he's got nothing better to do but ruin my life. I can certainly blame him. I blame him for never getting over anything..for being a prejudiced prick who doesn't think I'm good enough to be part of *his* family.

There's always Edgar too. I can blame him for getting me so angry that I lost it. It's his fault Catherine's been so different around me the last few weeks. I can see it when she looks at me..a feeling that lingers there like some secret that we don't speak about..just a flicker in the back of her eyes..a small part that sees me the same way all those rich brats at Academy saw me..dangerous..like a criminal just because my eyes are darker..because my skin isn't as white. Edgar put that look in her eyes. He wants her to see me that way just as badly as Hindley does. It's probably been his plan all along to drive her away from me like that.

—You're impossible— Nelly says.

—Yeah..and you're bothering the shit out of me— sitting up suddenly because I'm sick of her.

What does she know anyway?

Her and all her friends fall in love as easily as catching a cold..and they get over it just as fast. Nelly has no idea about us..about how me and Catherine need each other because our ghosts are like Siamese twins.

—You're not going to get rid of me, Henry— Nelly says, taking a seat next to me on the bed.. being as stubborn as she's always been. —I'm not leaving until we figure something out—

—There's nothing to figure out— I turn over on my back and take a deep breath.

—Do you have to be so negative all the time?—

—Why do you care so much?— propping my head up and almost shouting.

—Because! You guys are my friends.. and you make the perfect couple!— She's all smiles and quarter-moon eyes after that.. acting like she's wanted us together for the longest time when she's actually tried to set Catherine up with every snob in school.

—Is that what you told her about Edgar?— I mutter and her smile disappears just as quickly as it came.. her small eyes open as wide as they can and she puts on like I've offended her but we both know I'm only telling the truth.

Nelly gives up the act.. rolls her eyes and throws her hands down on the bed. —Okay. But that was before I knew being with him was a bad idea. He's got her thinking he's in love with her. Really, she's just the latest trophy for him. He'll get over her as soon as he knows he's won her. I don't want to see her get hurt. And besides, how was I supposed to know you liked her, liked her? I mean, I thought you liked her like a sister— kind of sticking her tongue out as she says it like she's still getting used to the idea. —It would've been creepy to think about that before.. but like everything's different now—

117

—It's always been different, you just didn't see it— I say.

—Yeah, I guess— Nelly says.. putting her hand under her chin and thinking about us.. about me and Catherine. —Ever since you told me, I can sort of see it. I mean you two have always been a little weird with each other— her thoughts drifting away when she tells me how romantic it is to think about.

—It doesn't matter— I mumble. —They've all turned her against me anyway. She sees me the same way everyone else does—

—What are you talking about?— Nelly snaps at me. —She's never looked at you like that, are you kidding? God! She likes you just as much. Or she did before you went all hermit and everything—

—Whatever—

—It's true. She's never thought that about you and you know it. You're just letting Hindley get to you, that's all!— She stands up.. her hands on her hips, saying I'm too full of self-pity to see it, and challenges me to snap out of it. —He's a creep, okay? You have to ignore him. Besides, for all you know, your real parents might be the king and queen of Mexico and you were kidnapped for ransom—

—Mexico doesn't have a king or a queen— I correct her.

—You get the point!—

—No. Not really— I say.

I make like I'm going to lie back down but she grabs my shirt.. her face growing red with her temper. —Don't be so dense!— she shouts.

—Fine. So what's your point, then?— I ask, only to get her to leave me alone.

—The point is, none of that matters. Not to Catherine anyway. All that matters to her is that you've been ignoring her and Edgar hasn't. She knows that he likes her, but you.. she's not sure you don't hate her!—

—Well, what am I supposed to do? I'm like a prisoner in here!— I yell.. not really at her.. yelling more because the frustration is finally getting to me now that I realize Edgar might actually be able to replace me.. that Catherine might be able to feel the same about him as she once did with me. And because I've been so afraid of Hindley, I've let it happen right in front of me.

—Go find her! That's what you're supposed to do— Nelly says. —Forget about getting grounded or whatever—

As much as she bothers me, I know she's right.

It doesn't matter anymore if Hindley throws me out on the street.. it can't be any worse. I thought so before.. thought being close to Catherine would be enough but it's not. If I let things stay like this, I'll lose her anyway. If I try, at least there's a chance we'll end up together.

—Okay— making up my mind to go through with it.. to give her plan a try. —Where is she? Is she at his house?—

Nelly shakes her head.. says they were going for a walk on the beach. I don't bother throwing on a sweatshirt or a jacket and rush up the basement stairs wearing just the T-shirt I have on. A little cold won't matter.. the only important part is getting there before I lose the courage to tell her everything.. tell her without saying a word because she'll understand as soon as I hold her.. as soon as our souls touch when I kiss her.

Frances tries to stop me when I rush by. —Where are you going?— she growls.. wrinkling her forehead and saying that the kitchen needs straightening.. that there's more to be done after that. Her face stretching into an ugly mix of anger and confusion when I ignore her. She starts getting up from the kitchen table but she's too slow.. holding her swollen belly in one hand and her sore back in the other. —*Hindley!*— she shouts.. giving up on trying to stop me.. tattling just like he would.. just as rotten as him and it's no wonder they ended up together.

My feet never break stride, though.

The door swings open and sets me free.. sprung from my cage.. my arms pumping as fast as my legs as I run around to the back of the house.. dip through the shrubs and along the rocky cliffs until I get to the steps that lead down to the sand.

The fog starts to break up and I can make out figures standing against the waves.. little kids with buckets of seashells and hoods drawn tight over their ears.. dogs on leashes pulling their owners onto the jetties.. and two more figures walking hand in hand. I can barely see them in the distance.. the fog keeping close to them.. draping them in purple clouds like clothes from Heaven but I know it's her. I know by the way the wind moves her hair.. by the shape of her ear sticking out slightly.. the one she used to cover with her hand whenever she could because some kid called her Dumbo in first grade and she never really got over it.

I bet Edgar doesn't know about that..bet he doesn't know anything important about her the way I do.

He has no right to be with her!

My feet move the sand out of the way..pushing it aside like fins flapping against the current..picking up speed..taking short quick breaths that seem to blow the clouds back into the sky as the sun begins to burn through..single rays shining like spotlights with one bright beam directly on them.

That's when I see them kiss.

That's when I stop running.

The sky is smiling on them..the waves crawling over the sand, stretching just far enough to touch them..the noise of the city vanishing for as long as they stay locked together and even the gulls stop their screeching to watch.

It all seems so clear then..seeing them together. I know now that my fate isn't the same as it used to be. I wasn't quick enough. The stars have already changed their mind. I'm almost sure of it.

SEVEN

*T*he entire Linton house feels alive as the guests move from room to room. The lights are kept dim. Laughter keeps the rooms bright. The high-pitched laughter of women in designer dresses when they toss their heads back. A flash of white teeth behind lipstick smiles and a casual wink as they bend their wrists to touch the last dangling end of a necklace, or a bracelet, or sometimes just a soft area of skin on their neck. Anything that attracts those around them and brings all eyes up to their faces.

The men laugh too. It's different, though. With them, it comes from deep in their throats. Almost like something they swallowed down the wrong pipe but still enjoyable somehow. They are different with their eyes too. They don't look up, they look down. Straighten the seam of their blazers or fidget with a pocket because for some reason it must be embarrassing to laugh as a man.

The whole scene reminds me of the parties my dad used to throw. Only he wasn't afraid to laugh. He loved the attention.

Being the life of the party. I never did. I preferred watching instead. Henry and I would sneak off into a corner or on the landing of the second floor where I could watch with my head peeking through the railing. It was like watching a fairy tale and my father was the storyteller who everyone else gathered around to hear his voice. I used to tell Henry how the women's dresses sparkled like stars when they caught the light the right way. He would smile and pretend to see it too, but I know he never understood why I thought it was so beautiful to watch. I didn't mind. Elegance is something that girls understand better.

I always felt apart from it, though. Like I never fit in any other way except as someone who observes from a distance. I tried to. Sometimes. I would practice smiling the way the women smile. Alone in my room, winking into the mirror and trying to make every boring comment sound interesting, but I always sounded dumb and plain.

Like a monkey trained to do human things, that's how I feel at these parties. I used to think it was because my mother wasn't around to teach me those things. Now I know those are the things you have to learn on your own, and I'm just not very good at them. Socially awkward. That's what Hindley used to say about me. My dad told me not to mind him. "You're special in so many more important ways," he'd say, but deep down I know he sort of wished I could be more like him. More the life of the party.

Isabelle is that way.

I've been watching her all night. Everyone has. The light blue dress she's wearing makes her eyes glow and her black curls fall in just the right places to frame them like the night. And she's perfect at getting attention. Even when her laugh is faked, people can't keep themselves from being enchanted by her. The women think of her as an adorable doll the way they fuss over her. The men all notice that she's very alive. Even the ones who shouldn't, they all stop to flirt with her in the innocent way she has of doing it so that she could never be accused of doing anything wrong.

I secretly wish I could be like her. Not in the spoiled way she acts, just in the way it comes so easily for her to be adored by strangers. I've been pretending all night that she's a princess. It doesn't take too much imagination given the way everyone dotes on her. But I've been elaborating on the fantasy a little. Pretending she's Anastasia and that this is the last ball before the revolution comes and turns the palace to ashes. I tell myself that I'm the only guest who knows they're coming. That they're just outside the gates, ready to break through the windows and drag away all the royal guests and that's why I have to stay near the back of the room. So I can make a quick getaway when the crashing comes. It twists my stomach into knots, thinking about it so much that it nearly feels real. That's why I practically jump out of my skin when Edgar taps me on the shoulder.

"You okay?" he asks.

"Fine," I tell him, taking a moment to let the images in my head dissolve into real life. "I was just.. being dumb," I say, giving him a goofy smile to apologize.

"Daydreaming?" Nodding as he asks because he's gotten to know me well enough lately to know all my worst habits. But that's okay, because the strange things I do only seem to make him like me more. And it makes me feel comfortable, like I don't have to hide who I am when I'm around him.

He never asks what I daydream about, and that's okay. I don't think he'd really get it if I told him that I was pretending his sister was Anastasia. It's funny how the act of daydreaming seems to make me cute, but the actual daydreams make me a little weird. That's why I don't mind it when he doesn't ask me to share them. I already feel out of place enough without going into some silly story I thought up.

His arms wrap tighter around me. His hands closing over my stomach and his chin touching my neck as he leans in to kiss me behind the ear. "Having fun?" he asks.

"Sure," I say, not sounding the least bit convincing. "I just feel a little like I don't belong," I admit.

Edgar just smiles. "Cat, you should never feel out of place. Especially not here . . not with me," he says. He touches my arm as he says it. His hands are electric and always make me glow. Then he leans in close to me again, whispering in my ear so that his words are warm against my skin. "You're my girlfriend, the rest of these people are just guests."

I turn my face toward his and place a kiss on his cheek to let him know it's sweet of him to say. "But there're so many people here," I tell him. "Strange people stand out more in a crowded room, didn't you know that?"

"So do the prettiest." His fingers move along my arm and over my shoulder as he whispers. They finally come to rest on my face, where he traces my freckles like he always does because he says freckles make me special and that I should show them off.

I tuck my lip under my teeth to keep from smiling too wide as his mother approaches us. She has her hands clasped in front of her and two guests following at her heels. "Here they are," she announces in a tone that playfully accuses us of hiding. "I want you two to meet some friends."

The next hour seems to be an endless flow of names and faces. Edgar is obligated to shake hands with every husband and son. I'm expected to exchange smiles and compliments with every wife and daughter. It's all very proper and planned, but there's still something about it that I find romantic. Something that always makes me remember dressing up in silly costumes and throwing imaginary tea parties with stuffed elephants when I was little.

Many of the people Mrs. Linton introduces us to knew my father. I know by the sympathetic look that quickly covers their initial smile. It lasts only a moment. Then they are bright and happy again, telling me what a great person he was and how he was always so proud of me. I know most of what they say is just polite conversation, but it makes me feel good to hear it anyway.

He'd be proud of me tonight too. Being shown off by Mrs. Linton. Treated like the center of attention and I'm actually going along with it and playing the part flawlessly. It's just like he'd always wanted. Only I have Edgar at my side and not Henry. That would be different for Dad to see, but I think he'd approve. All the people at the party seem to. We've become the cute couple that everyone loves to love.

By the time the evening is all over, I'm dizzy.

My brain is filled with the sounds of so many whispers. Hours and hours of them all being repeated at once. Comments that passed behind my back about how perfect Edgar and I look together. How beautiful I am and what a gentleman he's become. Even though it's so shallow, so much just about appearance because that's all that matters to them, it still sits inside me like something warm and safe that makes my cheeks blush.

I've already made up my mind not to tell Henry anything about it. He would roll his eyes. Rant and rave about how fake it all is. He'd get angry at me for letting myself get swept away by the glamour of a Linton dinner party. He'd be mad at them for attempting to brainwash me. He'd be mad at Hindley for helping them with the guest list. But mostly he'd be mad at me because when we were little and hid from these things, we made secret promises to never act like the grown-ups did. We'd run off and be savages if we had to, as long as we never had to learn which fork and spoon we were supposed to use first while seated like a lady and a gentleman.

There's still something exciting about the idea of living like that. Finding an island in the middle of the ocean and building a house in the trees. Living off coconuts and bananas. But that's a dream that can't ever really come true. But this one sort of can. At least for a few nights a year, I can live a fairy tale.

"Do you want me to walk with you?" Edgar asks once the night has changed over to early morning and the last of the people are getting ready to leave.

"It's only two houses away," I say with a smile, remembering the first day we spent together and how he asked me the same question then.

"So?" he says with a look in his eyes that's new for him lately. It's a look that goes right inside of him and through to the bottom. One that shows that he wants me more than anything else in the world.

"So," I say, same as I did that late afternoon weeks and weeks ago, only this time I'm ready to give him a different answer. I know he doesn't want to just talk and I don't want to talk either. I tilt my

head to the side, look at him through the top of my eyelashes, and
give him a shy look. "So . . . of course I want you to walk with me." •

> ⚡ ⚡

Hindley's rage is like lightning bursts in front of the sun . . blinding only for a moment and then it fades. I suffer through the flashes . . burned by them occasionally . . shielded from them other times . . but always just waiting for the calm that comes afterward.

It passes slower tonight than most nights.

He's worked himself into a rare form . . gone complete asshole . . spazzing out on anything and everything that crosses his path. I heard him swearing into the phone through the floorboards below me . . violent vibrations of an earthquake as he tore apart the room in a fit because whoever was on the other end wasn't letting Hindley have his way. Some poor piece of furniture took the blunt of it . . a chair or a small table . . maybe a lamp, though it sounded more solid than glass. He must have tossed it across the room from the sound of the crash . . sounded like a tree coming down in a thunderstorm . . the same snapping of broken wood and debris falling on the rooftops.

He's still at it . . a steady stream of objects hitting the floor . . being thrown against walls . . a constant rush of obscenities going off like fireworks. It's an extreme tantrum even for him. And once the furniture has taken its share of abuse, he'll come looking for me . . his favorite target . . the main event of all his liquor-fueled explosions.

I never know whether I should avoid him completely or just confront him and get it over with. Sometimes it's better to let him cool down. Other times, those quiet pauses are just the time it takes for him to refuel and that's when I find myself getting burned in a firestorm. It's always a gamble.

I debate it from behind the safety of a closed door. I haven't yet finished cleaning the bathrooms on the third floor.. a pointless chore since no one uses them, but Hindley seems to enjoy making me perform the useless tasks the most. There's a chance I can escape past his office without him noticing me.. take the heat for the bathrooms the next morning, if he can even tell that I never finished. There's a risk, though.. he catches me trying to slip past him and I'm stuck listening to him curse me out for what a lazy shit he thinks I am. Then he's guaranteed to rattle off a million other chores that will come at me like machine-gun fire. I'm certainly not in the mood for any of that.

My other choice is to finish what I'm doing and hope he isn't so drunk that he's waiting for me.. sitting in his office with the door open and a clear view of the stairs for when I walk by so he can summon me like a king seated on a throne.. like I'm no better than a slave under his control. Then it's worse.. harder to keep him from physically attacking me.. harder to keep myself from finally snapping and going after him. That would get me sent straightaway to some group home in Oakland that'll be ten times the shit hole that Bayside is. Being Hindley's servant sucks but not as bad as being the punching bag for fifteen kids who need to prove every day how hard they can be. At least here I still have a chance..at least I get to see her..as much as it hurts to see her, it's still better to hope for a few rays of sunshine than always living in permanent midnight.

I lean over the tub..place my cheek against the cool tile and try to think. I get a quick whiff of bleach before being interrupted by the marching charge of shoes echoing through the wall. Then a roar from the hall that decides my fate for me. Hindley screaming my name in a slurred accent.. shouting into every room he goes by because he can't even remember what idiotic jobs he's given me to do.

I stay still like a rat waiting to be trapped..my captor getting ever closer.

When he finally does drag himself through the door, I can tell by the redness in his eyes that my opportunity for an easy way out passed a few minutes ago..a few drinks ago. He's already over his limit..growling now instead of speaking.. leaning instead of standing..a meaner, sloppier version of himself. The only thing that never changes about him when he gets this way is how much he hates me..that's always in his eyes whether they're clear as the sky or bloodred.

He holds himself up..his hands on either side of the door frame to keep him balanced..looking down at where I'm kneeling near the toilet..a look on his face meant to tell me I'm no better than the shit he flushes down the pipes. —Stop wasting time— he sneers once he's able to form the words without stuttering.

—Fine with me— I stand up and kick the cleaning products across the floor..watch as the plastic bottles scatter like bowling pins and rub my hands together.

Hindley pushes himself off the wall and into a position somewhere between standing and falling. It takes all his energy to lift his head and glare at me.. shake his finger like talking to a small child and just once I'd like to show him how much I've grown.. make him feel it with my fist against his skull.. a beautiful chorus of cracking of bones.

—You know what really bothers me?— he says. —It's how lucky you are—

I give a short laugh at what a load of crap that is because from where I'm standing, it seems like luck has skipped me over. Hindley ignores me, though.. taking one step forward before continuing.

—Some immigrant slut pops you out easy as anything.. probably ten more just like you— He starts to sway as he talks.. getting into the imagined story of my life that he loves to tell.. recites it every so often like other people recite the birth of Christ.. like his hatred for me is something holy. —That bitch leaves you on the street like trash and my dad comes along and scoops you up.. gives you a cozy life.. sends you to the best school in the city.. everything you could ever want.. more than you people could hope to have— He leaves out the wicked stepbrother from his fairy tale.. all the parts that have me scrubbing bathrooms that are never used or clearing away dishes for guests.

—Whatever— I mumble.. blowing a stray strand of hair from my face. —I don't need to listen to this—

—But you do!— he barks.. straightening himself up to stand over me like a dictator. —Because now everything has to balance out. None of that was supposed to go to you.. your

132

life was supposed to suck. That easy life my dad gave you was meant for someone else . . someone who deserved it . . you took it from them and now they're going to have to make up for it—

—What are you talking about?— I mutter . . rubbing my eyes to hide that it's starting to scare me how he's not making any sense.

—I'm talking about MY goddamn child!— His eyes blazing like stars exploding when he shouts and slams his fist against the tile hard enough that it cracks . . a tiny splintering that quickly absorbs the trickle of blood coming from his knuckles . . leaving a thin red stain on the white porcelain. He shakes the pain away without a sound, but takes a few deep breaths before he can speak again . . getting each syllable out slowly. —The doctor says my baby will have a difficult time just being born . . that there might be complications for the rest of its life. That's your fault . . you stole that from my child—

—What?—

—You heard me— Hindley says with the calm of someone who's lost his mind . . believing all the mixed-up crap his brain is telling him. —You're going to pay it back, though. From now on, Frances has to stay off her feet . . you're going to make sure she gets everything she needs—

I refuse to listen to any more.

I head for the door but he grabs me . . pinning me in the doorway with his gasoline breath hovering in the air.

—You'll do what I tell you, you worthless spic!—

He's no longer a person when he gets like this . . nothing more than an animal with glowing eyes. These are the only moments that I'm afraid of him. The look he gives me burns through my skin . . melts the center of my bones and makes my blood feel like boiling metal. It makes me feel so weak, like a house made of straw . . one huff and puff and he can destroy me as simple as making a wish by blowing away the seeds of a dandelion.

I hate him for making me feel like that.

I hate myself too for even caring . . for putting up with it instead of just going away forever. But he knows I won't do that and that's what gives him this power over me . . lets him treat me like a little boy who he's big enough to pick on. It gets him off, I think . . he loves seeing me this helpless . . the way he smiles at having me caught between him and the wall . . to be able to call me names and knowing I won't dare talk back because he guards the only thing I ever wanted and he knows it.

—See you in the morning, Henry— he says once he's had enough of watching me behave like a coward. Then he stumbles through the hall . . steadying himself on the wall as he laughs to himself. I keep hidden in the doorway . . feeling the start of tears that I won't let show because that would be like admitting it even more that he can upset me.

I let my body slide down the door frame . . slipping onto the floor where the shadows cover me. Then I think of Catherine . . wishing she was next to me . . running her hands through my hair and telling me everything will be okay. If I think about it hard enough, I can almost hear the soothing sound of her voice. I can imagine the twilight shining through her bedroom window and pretend I'm lying on her bed . . breathing in the same rhythm as her.

But Hindley's made it clear that he won't let us write the ending of that fairy tale the way we used to dream about it ending. There's no happily ever after. . not for me.

Things won't go back to normal once that baby comes. The only thing that will change is that I'll be forgotten altogether. Catherine will have more social events to attend with Prince Linton and over time, I'll become nothing more than a servant that she feels obligated to say hello to. All I'll have left of what we used to share is the sour scent of her pillow that sits softly on everything she owns. Even that, I'll only have in small doses. . a passing memory that will fade over time.

EIGHT

*I look up from the magazine resting in my lap as Hindley comes
into the room. He's still shouting over his shoulder into the
hallway. Ordering Henry to hurry up. Complaining as usual. Saying Henry's too slow and that Frances can't wait all day.*

*It's been going for about a month now. Ever since the doctor
said Frances has to stay in bed, Hindley has been treating Henry
like her maid. Making him wait on her every second of the day.*

I'm sick of it.

*He's the one who should be doing all those things. He should be
getting her water every half hour. He should be rushing to her side
every time she calls out for whatever whim she decides on at any
given moment.*

*"You know, she's not his wife," I say, peeking above the glossy
advertisement promising clear skin so that I can glare at him.*

*Hindley doesn't see it that way. "If Henry wants to keep on
living here, he's going to have to earn it," he tells me.*

I throw the magazine aside and narrow my eyes. "You act as if he's a slave. He's not! He's part of this family," I shout.

Hindley turns away from the bar. He stops pouring his drink, pausing just long enough to give me the look he saves for when he wants to tell me to mind my own business. "Not anymore he's not," he says. "Over the last several weeks I think he's proven that he's just another delinquent." He turns his back to me again and continues to fill his glass with brown liquor that seems to swallow light, like some kind of poison that only makes him meaner. There's a clink of two ice cubes and then he sips. "I have to deal with that school calling every other day about all the fights he gets into. He's nothing but a headache."

I roll my eyes and shake my head.

"What did you expect when you sent him to that place?" I ask. I can't even imagine how bad it is there. Everyone knows Bayside is like the worst school in the city. As bad as jail probably. Thinking about Henry being forced to go there with those creeps makes me sick to my stomach. Hindley knew what it was going to do to Henry. It makes me so angry when I think about how unfair it is. "Maybe he's just sticking up for himself. Did you ever think of that?"

"Sticking up for himself? Is that what he did with Edgar out there on the lawn that time?" Hindley says.

He smiles when he sees my shoulders slump down. Grins even wider when I bite my lip and have nothing to say, then he lets a stifled laugh escape his lungs as he says, "That's what I thought."

"That was different," I mumble, but Hindley doesn't buy it. Truth is, I'm not even sure I believe it myself. Maybe Henry really has changed so much that I don't know him anymore. I can't be sure since he never talks to me. But that doesn't change the fact that it's Hindley's fault. He pushed Henry into being that way.

"Listen, sis, it's not open for discussion," he tells me with a wave of his hand, calmly pouring a second large drink into his glass.

He has some nerve! Dismissing me like he's my parent or something! He's not! He's still the same brat that he's always been. Only he's taller now and older and thinks he's got more say in things.

"I wish Dad were here! You know what he'd do if he saw the way you've been acting," I say.

Hindley finishes his second glass with one gulp and slams the glass down on the bar. Takes a deep breath that sounds like he's letting out fire from his throat the way a dragon breathes, then wipes his mouth with the back of his sleeve before glancing over at me like I'm the most annoying pest he's ever seen.

"Good for me then that Dad's not here," he says. "Too bad for Henry, though." A familiar hateful smile creeps across his lips, splitting his face in half as he shrugs. "His kind of people never get any breaks. I suppose that's fate."

"You're a jerk, you know that?"

I sink back into the sofa and fold my arms as I turn away from him.

Right away I'm wishing I'd thrown something at him like I first wanted. Something heavy. Something that would hurt him more than words because they have no effect on him. None except making him laugh harder. Laughing at me and then he comes over to the sofa, smirking away like he did when we were little and I was getting punished for something he tattled about.

"Silly Catherine, being a jerk is what makes me so successful," he says, straightening his suit jacket as he turns to face himself in the mirror. "You need to be clever to be a jerk. It takes skill. Any animal can be a brute like Henry. That's why he's the one carrying trays up and down the stairs and I'm the one heading downtown for a banquet." He exaggerates his gestures as he talks, trying to make himself appear important but he only comes off like a snob.

I glare at him as he walks past the fireplace and into the hall, where he takes one last look at himself in a smaller mirror that captures a softer light. There's a car waiting for him outside. A driver with a little cap whose only vocabulary is "Yes, sir." Hindley's so full of himself that I'm surprised he doesn't call Henry down from Frances's side to come open the door for him.

Dad was never like that.

Even with all of our money, he treated people like equals.

"I'll be home later this evening," he says to me.

"Do us a favor and don't bother," I say back at him.

He smiles and opens the door. He's so preoccupied with getting the upper hand on me that he doesn't notice Nelly barging past him. He nearly falls down on the porch when they collide. He leaves, swearing at Nelly, who is trying her best to apologize.

I tell her to never mind about saying she's sorry. "He's not mad at you," I say.

The door slams behind him and I can hear the angry marching of his steps across the floorboards and down the walk where the car is parked at the curb. Nelly stays by the front door, slightly stunned by the whole scene. Mostly, though, she's just confused by me because as soon as I hear the car drive off, I start rubbing at my eyes and sniffing up all the signs that I'm crying.

"Okay, are you going to tell me what's going on here?" she asks, throwing her handbag aside and sitting down beside me.

"Nothing," I say. "Just Hindley being the way he always is."

Nelly leans forward. She pushes away a strand of my hair that's gotten stuck against my cheek. "Want to talk about it?"

Before I can say anything, we hear Frances explode into one of her hysterical rants. Her voice sounds like a car accident. Like tires screeching on the pavement before the crash. "Are all of you people stupid, or just lazy?" she screams.

Henry's voice fires back, "Get it yourself, then! Lazy bitch." Then a door slams so hard that we feel the walls shake. Nelly's mouth falls open. Her hand moving quickly to cover her surprise at how he spoke to her.

"That pretty much says it all," I sigh. "No need to talk about it now."

Nelly frowns and her whole face seems to droop.

"It's gotten that bad, huh?"

"Worse," I answer.

Nelly and I haven't been talking much lately. Not about anything terribly important. Not any real conversations. Nothing more than passing hellos in the hallway or chatting at lunch. But then it's always a whole group. Not just the two us. Not like it used to be.

I guess it's my fault.

I've been spending so much time with Edgar that she and I have gotten lost. But that doesn't change anything between us. Not deep down. She's still going to be here for me now. When I need her. She's still my best friend.

"Is there anything you can do?" she asks.

"Doubt it," I say. "I've tried, but Hindley is so pigheaded he won't listen." Then I hesitate, because I feel guilty about what I'm going to say next. Well, not so much guilty, more sad, I guess. But I say it anyway because it's true. I tell her that Henry's not much better. "I don't even know if I should try to help him. He won't even look at me anymore, much less talk to me. It's like he hates me or something."

Nelly's eyes shrink to their smallest size and her voice turns slowly into a hissing sound. "You know that's not true," she says. "You're the one who's been avoiding him to spend all your time with Edgar," saying his name like it's some kind of swear word.

"What are you talking about?"

"YOU!" she snaps. "I'm talking about how you've treated Henry just as bad as everyone else since this crazy mess started. You've been acting like just as much of a snob as anyone else. You think now that Henry goes to Bayside, he's no better than any other kid that goes there!"

I move away from her in shock. Maybe I made a mistake. Maybe things between us really have changed worse than I thought because I can't believe she would accuse me of being like Stephanie and all those other gossipy friends of hers who go around telling everyone lies about Henry joining a gang or getting arrested. I'm the one who stopped being friends with all of them, not Nelly. I'm the one who argues with Hindley to ease up on Henry. How could she even say that to me?

"I don't have to listen to this," I say. "Besides, you don't even know what you're talking about!"

"Sure I do," she says. "You ditched Henry for Edgar because you didn't think he was good enough for you anymore."

"That's crazy!"

"You're telling me you weren't in love with Henry before?" she asks.

I feel my cheeks blushing, turning bright red at hearing my most private secret that I swore never to tell. Not even Nelly!

"See, I knew it," she says, nodding and pointing at me.

I turn away from her and stare out the window at the houses across the street.

I can't bear to look at her.

She must think I'm some kind of freak for ever liking Henry. If I look at her, I'll probably feel the same way. So I watch the way the sun makes the roofs appear to burn as it sets. "So what if I did?" I say. Talking to the sunbeams instead of her. Watching them turn everything to fire as I speak.

"The 'so what' about it is, why don't you anymore?" she barks.

I glance over at her and see she's not preparing rumors to spread or to cut me off from being her best friend. She's actually smiling at me, but not like before. Not like a teacher ready to give me detention anymore. She's smiling like normal now. Like she would if we were sitting up on my bed talking about any other boy in school and I guess that's her way of letting me know she doesn't think it's weird at all. That she sort of understands.

"I know it's not the same with Edgar. I can tell it's not same. You don't talk about him like you used to talk about Henry," she says, trying to make me admit that I still like Henry.

It's all too complicated to explain. The way Henry and I are is too much to think about sometimes. Edgar and I are easy. Nothing to think about or work at. Our bodies kind of take care of everything on their own. With Henry, I feel everything too much and it frightens me.

I slowly shake my head and frown. "It's different now."

"Different how?" she says, saying it in a way that lets me know she thinks I'm being unfair.

"It just is, okay?"

"No, it's not okay! You gave up on him," she says, accusing me like everything that's happened is somehow my fault.

I won't let her do that. I'm not going to take the blame for things I didn't do.

"He gave up on me first," I say, letting my hair fall just right so that she can't see that it gets to me. I know my eyes show it. Filling up with something sad once I start thinking about the way Henry shut me out. Nelly has no idea how much it hurt getting pushed away when I tried to help him!

She gently touches my arm. Like saying she's sorry for what she said, but thinks she had to say it anyway. "You do love him, though, right?" she asks. Her voice is softer than before and mine goes softer too.

"I don't know," I admit. I take a deep breath and slide my fingers over my face, tucking my hair behind my ear as I turn to face her. "I used to think me and Henry were like two parts of the same person," I tell her. "We kind of fit together that way. But I don't know anymore. The way we were with each other, it was like . . like maybe we were drowning each other, you know?"

I take a deep breath when I've finished. I've wanted to tell Nelly all of this so many times, but stopped just before letting anything slip. But it's easier than I ever imagined. I guess telling secrets is always easier once they're out.

"That's never what it sounded like to me," Nelly says. "It always sounded so perfect."

"It kind of was," I say. "But it kind of wasn't at the same time." It makes me sad to finally admit that. "It's different with Edgar. I don't feel any of those other things. I just feel . . . happy."

Nelly tells me that maybe love is more than just feeling happy.

"With how crazy things have gotten, maybe happy is really what I need right now," I tell her.

"Maybe," she says. "But he needs you." She tells me that I should give Henry another chance. That there's no reason it wouldn't be like before. But that's not true. Me and Henry can never have our secret world back.

"I can't," I say. "Sometimes I think about him . . . about how violent he can be . . . it kind of scares me." I can't believe I've said it, but it's true. It's how I feel. "It's all ruined now."

As my voice dies down, we hear Frances yell and I roll my eyes. I'm sort of relieved in a way too. It gives me a reason to change the subject. I'm still not comfortable talking about me and Henry. And I'm about to tell Nelly what a lazy cow Frances has been, how she's taken advantage of the doctor's concerns and milked it for all it's worth, when I hear footsteps outside the living room. Then the front door creaks open and closes quietly.

Nelly and I stare at each other.

My mouth drops open because I know it could only be Henry. My heart leaps at the thought that he might have been listening to us. I panic at the thought of him hearing only part of what we said. The wrong parts that would give him the wrong idea.

I jump up and hurry to the window.

I see him walking away from the house like a shadow with his head down. I tap on the glass because I want him to come back. I want to explain to him what I meant. I want to tell him that I do still love him. I never meant that I didn't love him, just that I love him differently now. But he doesn't turn around. He doesn't hear me or doesn't want to hear. Doesn't matter which, I need to stop him either way.

I hurry toward the door, ready to call him back inside. My hand is turning the knob and I open my mouth to shout but Nelly's screams take the place of my words. Her voice taking over the room before it breaks off into silence.

The next noise freezes me.

It's not Nelly screaming, but a dull echo that seeps in behind it. A rumbling noise like thunder falling out of the sky.

I follow Nelly's eyes and see Frances tumble down the last flight of steps before her body comes to rest a few feet in front of me. Her arms and legs are bent the wrong way. Her fingers twisted like bird feet behind her back.

And she doesn't make a sound.

She doesn't speak or move, she only bleeds.

The stain on her nightgown quickly spreads and I cover my mouth. I look back through the open door, wanting to see Henry running back but he's already gone. Too far for voices to travel. Part of me goes with him, leaving me paralyzed.

I stand there like a statue and it's Nelly who rushes to Frances's side. One hand on her shoulder and the other supporting her neck and asking over and over, "Are you okay? Are you all right?" before hurrying to the phone and pressing three numbers.

She tells my address to the person on the other side of the phone. She listens and nods when they tell her what to do until they get here. She does everything as I just stand there watching the red puddle grow larger. Unable to move or speak because *whatever was left of our family has just been pulled apart. Ripped in all directions and it feels like everything inside has been emptied out of me. And for a moment, I don't even realize that the screams filling the room are coming from me.*

⚜ ⚜

I balance the tray carefully to make sure nothing spills..not because I really care..I just don't feel like cleaning anything up if it does and I really don't feel like making another trip.

—You're sure taking your time with that— Hindley says from the bottom of the stairs..following my every step with his eyes..hounding me as usual. He doesn't even think I'm capable of doing the simplest task without him watching over me.

I'm tempted to turn around and let the tray fall..to toss it down on him and watch the silverware stab him in the eyes. Just the thought of it makes me smile. Knowing that I'll get revenge one day is what makes me able to keep going. He knows it too..that's why he leaves when he catches me looking at him. He's afraid of me. He's always been afraid of me. He should be even more afraid now. I don't plan on pretending to be his servant forever..it's going to end soon and then we'll settle all of this.

When I get to the top of the stairs, I use my foot to kick on the door and let Frances know I'm coming in. I don't know why she can't just leave it open. But I guess it makes her feel good about herself to have me knock..lets her imagine that

I actually work for her simply because she gets to say —you may enter—

A harder kick opens the door. It rubs against the carpet and I have to lean against it to push it open wide enough to squeeze through. Some of the soup spills in the process.. running down my arm and soaking the napkin. It's a mistake that Frances has been watching for. —Don't be so clumsy— she says, folding the blanket down over her lap as she sits up in bed.

I'm so used to her nagging that it's easy to let it pass.. get on with it and get out.. the less I have to deal with her, the better.

She points to the spot next to her where she expects me to place her dinner. She avoids looking at me.. keeping her eyes on the television instead.. mindless images flashing over her brain-dead gaze. —Put it down!— she barks. Then she gestures behind her back. —And prop up these pillows behind me— giving out orders as easily as breathing and I'm not sure which of them I want to kill more.. her or her husband.. they both deserve it.. they're both too selfish to be allowed to live.

I put the tray down but make no effort to fix the pillows when she leans forward. The doctor said she couldn't strain herself.. moving some pillows around is far from a strain even for someone as lazy as her. —You're not helpless— I sneer.

—Typical— she says.. leaning back again.. mumbling on about how uncomfortable she is.. how heartless I am because I can't see how sick she is. —You have no concern for anyone but yourself— she says.

I do my best to ignore her. She's only trying to get under my skin.

—Why they don't round all of you up and ship you back over the border, I'll never know— she mumbles . . rearranging the items on the tray . . placing the spoon on the opposite side of the bowl . . nudging the glass of water closer to the corner . . fidgeting with any little thing she can to emphasize how useless she thinks I am.

I just shake my head and start for the door.

—Where do you think you're going?— she shouts.

—I brought that up . . that's all I was told to do—

—Are all of you people stupid, or just lazy?— she screams . . running her hands through her greasy hair . . her eyes all bloodshot and frazzled . . finally looking as crazy as the ignorant rants she makes. —I . . need . . a . . new . . napkin— she says . . waving the slightly dripped-on one that I brought up . . speaking in pauses like talking to a three-year-old to make sure I understand.

That's it!

I'm done playing her game.

—Get it yourself, then! Lazy bitch—

I slam the door behind me . . silencing her gasp of surprise. It's going to get me in trouble . . days of it . . the vein in Hindley's forehead will stick out and his face will boil over with anger as he screams at me, but that won't be until morning, though . . I've already heard the car pull away. It means I'm free for the rest of the night. Frances is on her own.

I hear her calling my name . . a muffled shouting behind

the closed door. I don't pay it much attention, though. I've already started thinking about how I should take this time to talk to Catherine. With Hindley gone, it's the best chance I've had in weeks.

I need to straighten everything out with her..come clean once and for all. Hindley's not going to keep me hanging around here forever..much less than forever if I keep making scenes like the one that just happened.

There's no reason to stay quiet now.

I need to get her to come with me for a walk by the bridge..lie in the grass like we used to..watch the moon fight through the glare of the electric lights..just for a few hours..just long enough for her to remember that we're meant to be together.

I have to.

I head right for the living room..struggling to sort out all my nervous words..only thinking of what I plan to say makes me stutter even in my head and I stop on the second floor to get ahold of things. I don't want to stumble in there all sweaty and tongue-tied.

Her voice drifts up in a whisper and I can hear her talking to someone. I wait on the landing..holding my breath..listening..worried that it's Edgar and that I've missed my chance again because I'd never get even two words in with the way he smothers her. I need to know the situation before I barge in there, so I lean over the railing to bring myself closer to the sound of her voice.

—It's different now— she says and I dread the sound of the voice that will respond.

—Different how?—

It's only Nelly.

I start down again.. feeling lighter.. feeling more sure of what I want to say. I'm about to go into the room when I catch more of their conversation.. overhear Nelly asking Catherine if she loves him and I stop halfway between the first floor and the second. It should make me want to rush in there and interrupt them before Catherine can answer.. let her hear my side of the story.. try to change her mind if she's thinking of saying —yes— but I don't. I freeze for some reason. I guess, deep down, I want to know her answer before I even try.

—I don't know— she says and that means there's hope. —I don't know— means the future isn't decided.

But then, the rest of what she says kills any hope and makes me feel partially dead. Feels like I've been stabbed because I realize she's not talking about Edgar.. she's talking about me. She's telling Nelly that we used to fit together.. that we were meant for each other.. the same words she's told me so many times.. that the stars made it so we found each other. Then come the other words.. the ones she's never shared with me.. the ones that make me feel like dying inside. —But I don't know anymore.. the way we were with each other.. maybe it wasn't right—

She says being with me is like drowning.

She says it's different with Edgar. —I just feel.. happy— she says.

I lean against the wall.. feel my body slide to the floor.. feel my bones evaporate to dust because if that's how she feels, then I'm no better than a ghost already.

I listen to Nelly argue for me..telling Catherine that she's got it all wrong, but it's no use. Catherine actually tells her that I scare her! I used to be the one she'd run to whenever she got scared..now it's me she's running from? —It's all ruined now— Catherine tells her and nobody knows better than me that it's the truth..that *now* everything is ruined.

The floorboards above me begin to creak as Frances starts calling my name louder..screaming it almost in a panic but it matters even less to me than it did five minutes ago. I pull myself up and head for the front door.

I have to get away. The walls are strangling me..squeezing me so thin that I'm going to be crushed..making me blind until I hurry out into the breeze..managing to escape just in time as I run into the night that has settled over the street..touching on everything and it feels like a friend..feels safe. I want to disappear into it..vanish completely..so I hurry away, keeping my head down..letting the shadows hide me.

Frances's cries chase me until they get swallowed by the streetlights and evaporate with distance. I hope they have the same power over the things Catherine said..hope the electricity can make them fade as I run faster..farther..hoping to get somewhere where all of this begins to feel like a dream that I won't be able to remember in the morning.

It's not working like that, though. The sound of my shoes drumming against the sidewalk gets distorted..turns into words..her words..repeating themselves and even when I throw my hands up to cover my ears I can still hear it playing back. I can hear her in my bloodstream..my pulse borrows

her language..says what she said..saying it louder..
faster..twisting it around so that the words get meaner as I
turn off our block and into the park where the wind rushes
through the trees..the rustling branches quickly joining the
chorus screaming in my head.

—Shut up!— I shout and try to outrun them.

—*Shut up!*— shouting it silently in my head..trying to
drown out the other voices..shouting it in a whisper under
the wind all along the path. —*Shut up*— for nearly a mile
until I get near the bridge and collapse in the grass..too out
of breath to shout anymore. Slowly, the other voices begin
to stop. They get washed out of my mind by the sound of
waves crashing against the rocks..by the whistling of the
tall grass swishing around my head and the sound of a million ants buried alive in the ground.

I look up at the metal towers reaching into the sky and finally start to slow down. The blinking lights, meant to warn
off helicopters and planes, steady my nerves as I switch my
eyes to their frequency..letting the rhythm take over..on
then off..on then off..and I adapt my lungs to the pace..
letting the hum of traffic sing me a lullaby.

I let my head sink into the soft dirt..watch the clouds
move in over the hills across the bay..moving quickly.. moving like smoke from a wildfire that blocks out the sky but
with the smell of rain instead of the smell of burning
ground. The clouds pass each other..collide and scatter..
their outlines getting confused until there is only a storm
blanket reflecting back the purple electricity of the city.

—Could she really have said that she's afraid of me?— I

mumble . . asking the bridge . . or maybe the wind because it seems so unreal to think of her saying it that they seem as likely as me to have an answer.

Me and Catherine used to be like the clouds covering the bay . . so close that it was impossible to separate us without tearing the other to pieces. But that's exactly what they've done . . Hindley and his wife . . they've split us apart like wind ripping clouds into fragments so that the broken bits don't fit together anymore. They've ruined us so much that Catherine doesn't even recognize me.

Everything she said was their fault. They kept pushing me until I snapped . . like poking a dog with a stick and then when it bites, they point and say —We told you so . . told you he was dangerous—

It's not fair!

They shouldn't be able to do this to me. They shouldn't be allowed to take her away just because they want to.

I pound my fists on the ground . . dig my fingers into the grass and strangle the roots . . thinking about how I'll destroy everything that's important to them . . how I can make their lives miserable too . . because if there's no chance for me to be happy, I won't let them be happy either.

⋈ ⋈

When the phone finally rings, I'm not ready. It's been two hours, maybe three since I started staring at it. Squinting my eyes like somehow I could make it ring if I concentrated hard enough. But my mind must have wandered. The steady rain tapping against the windows distracted me and now the ringing startles me like the blaring of a fire alarm.

Then I start to remember why I've been waiting. It comes streaming back to me. Frances falling. The ambulance sirens flashing like Christmas lights through the front door. The frantic message I left for Hindley telling him to hurry down to St. Mary's Hospital. All of it swims around in my head and hits me at once.

Hindley should've called before now.

If everything were okay, he would have called already.

I move automatically, pushing the chair away from the kitchen table and walking like a zombie across the tiles. My hand makes the phone stop screaming with the press of a button and a shiver runs along my spine as I raise it up to my ear. "Hello?" I say, barely loud enough for anyone on the other end of the line to hear. But someone does. Someone clears his throat to greet me.

It's Hindley.

He doesn't have to say anything for me to know it's him. I know it just by the way he sighs. And by the tight sound he makes as he swallows, I know it's not good news.

"Is she okay?" I ask.

I can almost hear him shake his head.

"No," he utters softly.

I should be with him. I should be at the hospital. They asked me if I wanted to ride in the ambulance as they carried her out the door. I couldn't, though. My legs wouldn't move. My mouth wouldn't work. All I could think about was the blood drying on the floor and they left without waiting for me to answer. Everything moved in such a rush. Everything except me.

I was stuck. Something like being paralyzed, I guess.

It's the same way now.

I feel my body go weak listening to Hindley explain how they had to take the baby early. Putting my hand up to my mouth in shock as he tells me how they had to cut it out of Frances's stomach because she was dying and her dying was killing the baby. He says they had to save one from the other. That only one of them could live and the baby had the best chance so that's what they did.

The more I listen, the more it begins to feel like it isn't happening. Like the conversation we're having is happening between ghosts and I'm only eavesdropping.

"Damn it, Catherine! Enough!" Hindley suddenly shouts.

I wasn't even aware I was saying anything until Hindley told me to stop.

I'm still saying it, though.

The words are coming out of my mouth by themselves. The same three words. "Oh my God. Oh my God," whispering it through my fingers and I only know that I finally stop because the warm breath doesn't touch my palm any longer.

"I don't want to hear it," he says. There's something ugly in his voice when he tells me again to be quiet. When he tells me never to mention God again. "Not around me," he says in a violent tone.

"Hindley . . ." I stutter, struggling to find words.

I want to tell him I'm sorry. I'm so sorry for him. I want to tell him but it doesn't come together in time. The words take too long to form in my mouth and he hangs up. Disconnects the line and no matter how many times I try, I can never get him back on the other end. None of it feels real, though, until the dial tone fades away and I'm surrounded by nothing but quiet.

I start to feel dizzy. The tiles on the floor seem to spin in oppo-

site directions from the tiles on the wall and I stay perfectly still in the center like the chandelier hanging from the ceiling. There's too much space in here. Too empty and it's starting to swallow me into it. Like I'll vanish if I don't grab on to something. My heart's beating too fast, like a rabbit's, and all I want to do is curl up on the floor. Slow everything down because lately my life has been moving too fast to make sense of it.

"Is everything all right?"

The voice startles me. It's not Nelly. She's been asleep on the sofa for the last hour. Besides, this voice is weaker than hers. Quiet like a ghost that doesn't want to be heard.

A shiver passes through me when I see Henry standing on the other side of the room. His face is half hidden behind the doorway as he leans against the frame. One foot ready to leave while the other is ready to come toward me like he hasn't made up his mind which of them he's going to obey.

I decide for him.

I hurry across the room, fold my arms around him, and bury my face into his shirt. I don't care about all the things that have gone on between us the last few months. Right now I just want to forget about all of that. About everything. I just want things to be the way they were before.

In his arms, things start to slow down.

I can breathe again. I feel safe again surrounded by the scent of rain on his clothes. "I'm so glad you're here," I say. I mean it too. I need him with me when I go to the hospital. I need him next to me. His body presses against mine so close it's like we're folding into each other. He can make me stronger. Make the whole thing survivable. He's always been the best at making me feel stronger.

I hold him tighter, hoping for him to hug me back, but his arms stay at his sides. And when I look up at him, he's not looking at me. He's staring off at the window. Staring with such blank eyes that I start to wonder if he's really even Henry anymore or if he's changed so much that I can never have him back.

"Don't you really wish Edgar was here?" he asks. There's a different look in his eyes than any I've ever seen there before. A cold one. Almost like the rain has gotten inside and washed away part of him.

"Henry, please don't," I beg. I don't want to choose. Not now. Not tonight. "Please."

"Don't what?" he shouts. He pushes me away and runs his hand through his hair. He won't look at me. Staring at the floor and then the ceiling. Staring everywhere except at me. "I don't even know what's going on," he says, taking another step into the hallway. "Last I heard, I made you feel like you were drowning. Now you're all acting like this? What am I supposed to think? What is it you want from me?"

I grab on to his shirt. Keep him from walking farther away. He half tries to shake me off but stops once I manage to tell him about Frances. Getting it out in one breath and hoping that explains why I'm being the way I am and why I need him. I search his expression for any sign that he does, but there's nothing. Like he didn't hear me. Or didn't understand. Maybe both, so I tell him again. Slower this time. "She's dead, Henry," I say.

He doesn't ask me when.

He doesn't ask me how.

"So?" is all he says. Says it like I've just told him that he missed dinner or that I broke a glass. Saying it the same way he'd say "so" to any unimportant piece of news that he couldn't care less about. Then it's my turn to take a step away from him because I don't know what to say. I don't know how he could be so unfeeling. I know she wasn't very nice to him, but still she's dead. Dead is dead! It's not like being sick. It's not a fair punishment for her being mean.

And the baby?

He didn't even ask!

He only stands there with his arms out to his side, still waiting for me to make a choice between him and the rest of the world. Even now. Even with the stains of the accident still smeared over the hall, nothing matters to him except the pretend world that we used to live in. It doesn't exist anymore, though. We can't always hide from real life even if we want to.

He starts to walk toward the basement door. Backing away and shaking his head slowly like shaking the seconds away on a countdown. Giving me from now until he goes down the stairs to make up my mind.

"Aren't you coming with me to the hospital?" I ask.

"Why would I?" he mutters.

"For me," I say. I can't believe he would leave me alone. Even if he doesn't care about anyone else, he could at least do it for me. He could at least pretend. Because I need him. He's part of the family. Our family needs to be together tonight or it will die too. But I guess he doesn't care about that because he just keeps walking.

"I'd better not. I wouldn't want to scare you," he says.

He's trying to hurt my feelings like I hurt his earlier. He can't see that none of that matters anymore.

He heads down the stairs without turning around again.

"Henry!" I call out to him. "You know that's not what I meant! I'm sorry. This is different now. Henry?"

The sound of the rain is the only answer I get.

I wait for a minute. I cross my fingers and wait, but he doesn't come back. Part of me wants to follow him and make him understand, but I know Hindley needs me more right now. Henry knows that too, he's just being selfish. I can't deal with that now. Not with everything else. Maybe Nelly can make him understand when she wakes up.

I head out the door, still hoping he might meet me there later.

꿍 꿍

I lose track of time listening to the noise of traffic competing for space with the waves..with the wind rushing through the trees before covering me like a blanket. Somehow it's able to drive out all the thoughts that bothered me and I'm able to drift off. Not sure for how long..two hours.. more, maybe..at least as long as it took the first drops of rain to fall and wake me from my trance.

I let the water touch my face first..the bare skin on my arms..let it seep into my clothes as it starts to pick up. I begin to move with it..getting to my feet and heading back toward the lights that twinkle in the windows of the buildings in the distance..pausing for a second to watch the stream of headlights flash against the falling raindrops. It makes them look like a swarm of fireflies crashing against the asphalt as the storm gets stronger and I realize that I am like the storm.. like the swirling clouds and roar of thunder.

My thoughts are no longer like the little waves on the bay.. now they are angry like the sheets of rain beating against the cars.. more like the rushing streams washing trash through the gutters.. like a shattered wave violently thundering over the city and spraying down like machine-gun fire as I walk through it with a flash of lightning in my throat ready to strike as I turn onto Sea Cliff Avenue.

I stand on the corner, staring at the house I've grown up in. It looks cold and dead. I can't see the warm glow of the windows. It doesn't look anything like Heaven anymore as the rain sinks through my skin.

For the first time in my life, it doesn't feel like home.

I drag myself up the porch stairs.. struggle to shake off a flood of memories.. flashes of when things were different and somehow I wish I could stop time and stay in a place when nothing interfered with the way I thought the world should behave. And I head for the basement.. for my bed, where I can lie down and close my eyes.. let the images in my head slowly replace reality and pretend.

I stop, though, when I pass by the kitchen and see Catherine standing in there by herself.

I stay invisible so I can watch her.. hiding behind the wall and peeking in only enough so that I can see the way she stands with her hand on her lips.. the phone pressed to her ear. Only the smallest sounds come out of her mouth like the sounds she makes when she's asleep and dreaming.. perfect like an angel when she doesn't know anyone is watching her.. so beautiful without trying.

She used to smile if she caught me spying on her. It made

her happy to have me with her even when she believed she was alone. It's not the same anymore, though. Her smile isn't so secret anymore. I've seen her give Edgar the same smile. It doesn't belong to me anymore. Her smile can only belong to one person at a time and it's his now.

When she places the phone on the counter, I shuffle my feet to let her know I'm there before I ask —Is everything all right?—

She spins around slowly like a ballerina .. her arms bent at the elbows and held close to her body. Her hair catches the light from the chandelier when she twists .. turning the electricity into something softer like starlight.

My hands slide down the frame of the door and I make to walk toward her but she moves first .. coming toward me because she's always been the one to take the lead and I've always been the wave struggling to keep going forward as the ocean pulls me back.

Her arms help to keep me steady .. wrapping around my waist where her fingers lock together against the small of my back. She hides her face against my chest .. holding on so tight that I can feel her heart against my rib cage .. pounding faster now that we're touching.

—I'm so glad you're here— she whispers .. the sound of her voice muffled by my shirt but I can feel her breath .. a warmth that seeps through the soaked fabric and makes me shiver.

Outside, the wind picks up .. howling against the windows like the roar of the tide rolling in .. a strong wind that's blowing off the breakers like the one that lifted the fog that first time I caught her holding Edgar on the beach, the same way she's holding me here in the kitchen. I never forget that image. It never goes away..hangs around like the leftover feeling of a nightmare after waking up.

It's all I can think about as she holds me.

It ruins everything just knowing that she ever held Edgar like this. It's like somehow it no longer means the same thing to me as it used to. Her hands crawling over my shirt feel like the hands of a stranger..almost like she's touching him instead of me. The only reason she's not is because I happen to be here at the moment when she apparently needs someone.

—Don't you really wish Edgar was here?— I say because I refuse to be her second choice.

—Henry..please don't— she says. —Please— All the familiar traces of sunshine are gone from her eyes. The connection between us is gone too. It's almost like she doesn't recognize me when she looks at me.

—Don't what?— I bark at her. —I don't even know what's going on— I mumble as I'm stepping away from her. —Last I heard, I made you feel like you were drowning. Now you're all acting like this? What am I supposed to think? What is it you want from me?— I shout because it's starting to piss me off. The way she's treating me..the way she sees me like I'm the one who's done all the changing.

She's changed too!

I've seen the way she is with him..how they talk about expensive cars and getting invites to all the big parties..all the stuff we used to think was so stupid. Suddenly she finds it so fascinating. I've heard laughing about who's wearing what.. about who's dating who this week.. things that were never important to her before. She's turning into one of them.. into another snob from the Heights and she doesn't think I notice. Then she says those things about me to Nelly.. making me sound like some thug and then still expecting me to always be there for her.

She's wrong if she thinks I'll take everybody's abuse and wait around for the few moments when she needs me. I won't be a stray dog for her, holding out for scraps. It's all or nothing.. she has to decide. She's starting to get that too. It shows now that she tucks her bottom lip under her teeth. Her eyes begging me not to leave, but I won't let her manipulate me.

I run my hand through my hair and glance up at the ceiling.. at the floor.. at the rain streaming down the window.. staring anywhere but at her because if I do, she'll be able to change my mind. One perfect look from her and she could make me walk off the end of the world if that's what she wanted from me.

I force myself to walk away.. taking one step and then another.. retreating from a million mistakes that are waiting for me if I don't.

She doesn't let me leave so easily, though.. clutches at my shirt and pulls until I stop.

—Frances is dead— she says. Her voice trembling.. her hands shake slightly as she brings them up to her mouth again and she actually seems sad. —She's dead, Henry— she repeats.. her tone pleading with me to feel the way she does. But I can't.. not about Frances. Neither should she.. not for such an awful person who looked down on everyone even though she was nothing but trash who married rich.

Maybe it's Hindley who she feels sad for. But he deserves worse for the way he's been. In fact, it almost makes me smile thinking about Hindley by her bed, screaming at the doctors and nurses and knowing there's finally something he can't control..something he can't change just by bullying people around..learning that fate works in reverse too.

—She's dead— Catherine tells me a third time because I can tell she's not sure if I heard..not sure that it's sunk in yet because I'm not upset.

—So?— I say and she knows what I'm asking..asking whether or not it makes a difference..whether or not we can go back to being the way we were before now. It should be an easy answer but she doesn't seem to be able to make up her mind.

I start to back away..shaking my head at the thought of her even having to consider anyone else over me. She never would've before. But I guess it's like she said earlier..everything is ruined now. So forget it! I turn around and leave her there..let her figure it out on her own.

—Aren't you coming with me to the hospital?— she asks.

—Why would I?—

—For me— she says like it's the most obvious thing in the world. And maybe it was at some point but not anymore.

—I'd better not— I tell her. —I wouldn't want to scare you— I add just before disappearing down the stairs into the basement, where the rain is starting to seep through the cement walls. And my words make a direct hit. She tries calling me back..tries apologizing for the things she told Nelly, but that doesn't change the fact that she meant it.

Then there's a minute of silence that makes me wonder if she's going to come after me. But the front door soon opens and then closes above my head and I know I'm alone..that she's not picking me.

I close my eyes and let my body fall onto the mattress. So many different thoughts start screaming in my head and I cover my ears..pressing down as hard as I can..hoping to quiet them..or force them to come one at a time so I can make some sense of it.

I count each breath out loud until the numbers take over..counting until there's nothing else and I can finally open my eyes..keeping the lights off and letting the passing traffic make patterns on the wall..little electric rodents that scurry away in the blink of an eye. I chase them away with one glance but can't chase away the last thought that won't go away..the one telling me that she still cares about me but that she cares like a friend.

And I don't know if I did the right thing, but I do know that being friends isn't enough..that it shouldn't be enough for her either.

NINE

*T*here's a certain way everybody expects you to act after some-thing terrible happens in your life. You're supposed to be quiet except to cry. You're supposed to walk through the halls with your head down. You're supposed to sit in the back of every class-room, way back in the corner so that everyone has to turn around and peek at sadness without having it disturb them. And when a whole series of bad things happen to you right on top of another, people expect you to be even more tragic. That's how the kids at school want me to be because it's the way things are supposed to work. I should always be ready to break down at any given mo-ment because I'm supposed to be so fragile. And I guess I go along with it because it's easier than trying to make them understand that what I really want is just to be treated like nothing has hap-pened.

That's asking the impossible, though. With all the rumors go-ing around, it'll be a miracle if anyone treats me like a normal human being ever again. My life's become the school's favorite topic of gossip. The whispers follow me from classroom to classroom, passed from locker to locker and getting more outrageous each time they're repeated, like that playground game played by little kids at recess. Everything gets lost in the translation and somehow the story about what happened to Frances turns into rumors about Henry killing her.

The current version going around Academy is that Henry killed her because she found proof that he killed my father too. They've turned him into some murderous character straight from the pages of one of the Shakespeare plays we're always reading in English class. Uncontrollable and deranged and everyone saw it coming. Even the school supposedly. They bring up the time during freshman year when he mouthed off to our homeroom teacher for separating our desks. They talk about the time he hit this kid who was teasing me as some kind of missed warning sign. That's why they're all saying now that he was expelled. And depending on who you hear the story from, he also stabbed Nelly the same night. Though anyone who has seen her knows she was never injured.

Not physically anyway.

I'm not so sure how she's doing otherwise. I think she's fine, but I haven't really talked to her, though. I've kind of been avoiding her, because if I see her, I'll have to talk about what happened. I'll have to think about how my family splintered apart that night. How we keep moving further away from one another. Hindley drowning in his world of drinking and sinking deeper with each empty bottle. Henry staying hidden away in the basement. If he's even there, that is. Most of the time he doesn't even come home until late. It's like there's only me and the baby living there now. The only words that are spoken are between me and the babysitter, who leaves as soon as I get home.

Nothing feels the same.

Even I'm different now.

Nelly will be able to tell. That's part of why I've been avoiding her. She's been my best friend forever and I'm worried it's not going to be that way anymore. I'm afraid of what I might see reflected in her eyes when she looks at me. I'm afraid I'm going to lose her too. I guess that's stupid. I mean she'll probably be there for me no matter what. But that doesn't keep me from wishing I was invisible. Or that I could snap my fingers and speed up time. Get past all the uncomfortable conversations. Of course I can't, though. The best I can do is try to avoid all eye contact as I walk through the hall. Besides, that's what everyone expects from me anyways. Even Nelly, I suppose.

I'm still dragging my feet toward the cafeteria when the late bell rings. Watching my shoes and never glancing up at the stragglers running by and cursing because they're late for class. I'm only going to lunch, so it doesn't matter. I can be as late as I want. And the later, the better. That way everyone will have taken their seats and I can find an empty place to be alone.

I ignore the stares as I walk to the back of the room.

With all the noise, I can't hear what anyone is saying but I can tell by the pointed fingers and covered mouths that a lot of what is being said is about me. That's why the first thing I do when I sit down is cover my ears. Not in any obvious way. I make it look like I'm reading a magazine and simply using my hands to hold my head up. It's enough to muffle the roar and pretend I'm somewhere else.

I've been doing that a lot lately. Drifting off. But it's not like I used to. It's not like daydreaming. I'll be sitting somewhere and all of a sudden it's like I'm not there. And when I come out of it, I won't remember thinking about anything. It's like those minutes never happened.

I've started to look forward to it. Time passing along without me. I spend most classes staring out the window. Let my eyes go out of focus until the sky becomes a soft blue blur. The windows in the cafeteria aren't very good for that, though. They're too high on the walls and don't give any real view to the scenery. Plus the lights are too bright. And there're too many kids moving around. Too many distractions for me to be completely lost. But close enough. So close that I don't see Edgar standing in front of me until he coughs to get my attention.

"You okay, Cat?" he asks.

The sun shines in through the window behind me, directly on him like a blinding halo. It bleaches his face so bright that I can't see him clearly. But I can make out enough to know he has his eyebrows raised. His eyes are studying me to see if I have a fever or something and it's obvious that he's asked me the same question several times already before I noticed.

"Huh?" I mumble. "I wasn't paying attention."

A cloud passes in front of the sun for a moment. My eyes adjust to the shadows. Edgar's face comes into focus and I can see that he's worried about me. About how I've been acting stranger than normal. He tries to hide it, though. He shrugs it off. "Don't worry about it," he says. Then he steps around the table so that he can sit next to me.

When I don't say anything to him for an entire minute, he asks me if I want him to leave. I can tell he's hurt. He thinks he's done something wrong because I didn't look for him when I came in. "No. Stay," I say. But it comes out so slowly and so sad that it sounds like a lie. It sounds like what I really want is to be left alone, so he starts to get up.

"I'll go," he says.

I reach for his hand, closing it in both of mine, and force a smile. "Don't. I'm sorry," I tell him. "I'm just kind of out of it."

"You sure?" he asks, like he's waiting for me to change my mind. Letting me know with one look that he doesn't want to stay if I'm going to get crazy.

"Yeah, I'm sure," I whisper and he sits down.

Most boys would have ditched me altogether by now, but Edgar's been doing his best to understand. He's the only one who hasn't acted like I'm contagious.

"You holding up?" he asks, squeezing my hand tighter.

I shrug my shoulders. "Don't know," I say. "Why?"

"Just wondering," he says. "Actually, a bunch of people were wondering."

"Yeah?" and I can tell it bothers him. Not like it used to bother Henry. Henry would get angry and mean with them. With Edgar, it bothers him differently. He cares about what they think. He doesn't want to be known as the boy who's dating the freak.

"You sure?" he says. Wanting me to snap out of it. To act more normal because the strange little things that he sometimes likes about me have gotten to be too much today. Crossed the line from cute and over to strange. "All day, it's been like you're not even here."

I stare off into the sea of tables where people's heads bob up and down like waves. They seem so far away. Even the ones just across the aisle. "It sort of feels that way," I say, giving a short laugh to make it sound less serious than it feels.

"Maybe you should go home," Edgar tells me as he turns in his chair and slides closer to me. His arm slips behind me, wraps around my waist, and I let my head come down slowly to rest on his shoulder. "You know, come back when you're more yourself."

I take a few deep breaths and watch my ribs rise and fall. His hand is placed just under my breasts and I see the way his fingers seem nervous each time they almost touch when I exhale. I try to sink lower with each breath. Getting closer and closer. It makes tiny sparks crawl over my skin like electricity running through my veins. Makes my bones go weak too. Makes me feel more like myself than he could know.

I bring my face closer to his, holding a smile until we kiss. Keeping my eyes open so that I can see how the blue in his eyes borrows color from the sky, getting brighter just before being covered by the soft skin of his eyelids. Sharing a perfect moment before the chaos of the lunchroom intrudes and we separate.

Edgar opens his mouth like he wants to say something but every attempt ends in a false start. Because I know what he really wants is for me to say something more. He wants me to tell him that I'm okay. It's something I can do for him. A little thing, really.

"I'm fine," I say, putting my fingers near my mouth so that I can still feel where his lips were on top of mine. Just a trace of him. Like a ghost with the tiniest weight that stays with me.

"Cat, you have to try and pull yourself together," he says after our hearts settle back down. "Not for me. But for everyone else," he quickly adds. Too quickly.

I lean against him and shrink away from all the kids circling the room. I point at all of the faces, never taking my hand away from my mouth. "Why?" I whisper.

"Well . . . I mean if you ever want them to leave you alone about this, you have to act like you're over it," he says.

I know he's right. But I guess I don't really care so much about what anyone else thinks as long as he's here. As long as there's one person in the world who still pretends I'm fine. I've always been that way. Capricorns are like that. Strong most of the time, but they always need someone to lean on. For years it was Henry. All through elementary school and junior high and even last year. But Henry's as much a Pisces as I am a Capricorn. All fish swim off after a while.

Sometimes I wish I was a little more like that. Able to get away. Go someplace where nobody knows me. "Did you ever just want to be somewhere new?" Wondering aloud if Edgar ever felt the same way.

"What are you talking about?" he asks and I tell him it doesn't matter. "I guess," he says then. "Doesn't everyone?"

I watch the table of girls next to us. Identical faces with identical clothes as they pass secrets to each other with corresponding expressions to dictate the appropriate responses. They're so wrapped up in their high school games that they don't ever think about anything real. "Not them," I say. "People like that never want to be anywhere except for where they are."

In a way, I think it must be nice to be so unaware.

Edgar puts his other arm around me then. He locks his hands together across my stomach. "What are you talking about?" he asks and I know I've said too much.

"Nothing," I say. "Forget it."

He blows the hair away from his eyes and shakes his head. I squeeze his hands tighter in mine and bring him back to me. Bring us back to the easy place we like to be because I don't really want to talk about anything anyway. I just want him to hug me tighter so I'll believe he really understands me.

⚓ ⚓

I keep my head down on the desk.. my arms folded like a pillow.. one eye peeking out above my elbow to watch the skinny second hand spin around the clock and tick off the last minutes of detention.. tapping my sneakers as it passes the twelve and starts another trip.

It makes me crazy sitting in here.. only the one window, which looks out on a brick wall no more than ten inches away.. the space between the school and the next building is only a narrow chute reaching from the ground to the sky. It doesn't help bring any light in.. always gray even on a bright day like this.. same as being in the basement at home and it's like I'm cemented into a tomb every minute of every day of my life. Lately it's beginning to make me want to explode.

The teacher assigned to this room pokes his head up from the papers he's grading.. gives me a long stare with his beady eyes.. points at my feet and tells me —This isn't band practice.. how about keeping it down?—

Two kids in the back of the room snicker.. lean closer to each other and cover their mouths as they whisper.. laughing louder until I turn my head.

They fall silent once I stare at them.

The kids in this school treat me different now that I've got a reputation for fighting back..for hurting kids worse than they can hurt me. I got nothing to lose anymore..no reason to behave myself..no reason to worry about what happens. If I get expelled..if Hindley throws me out..none of it matters because my life is going to suck anyway. So when anybody starts acting like they're tough, I'm not afraid to attack them first. It doesn't matter to me if I get my ass beat. I don't care if four of their friends jump me later in the day. I don't care about anything and that's why most of them have backed off because not caring is what makes me a threat.

That's how I got in here today..and yesterday..pretty much every day the last two weeks. Just going for it and waling on kids that waled on me the first month I was here. I got so sick of everyone else making up rules for me..Dominican kids telling me that Mexicans aren't allowed to use the bathrooms on the third floor..Puerto Ricans telling me I can't use the lockers in the gym unless I ask permission first..black kids telling me Latinos aren't allowed to sit at certain tables unless I'm dressed right. I'm sick of that shit. They're no better than those people in the Heights with all their rules. So I stopped following them..started making enemies..started ending most every day in this room serving detention.

Five minutes left until the end of my sentence.

I flip through my notebook, trying to kill some time.. notice a few sketches in the front that I did for Catherine on my first day at Bayside. A bunch of black birds in a white paper sky..a stupid waste of time. I rip them from the spiral metal spine in one motion..crumple them into a mess and leave them on the floor by my feet. I can't believe I ever thought they'd change anything.

The next time I glance up at the clock, it's thirty seconds past the end of detention. —Hey! Time's up— I say.. banging on the desk with my knuckles. The teacher looks up at me and I point to the clock.

He pushes his glasses up from the tip of his nose and gives the clock a disinterested glance. —Go on, leave, then— he says and goes back to grading papers without another thought.. dismissed like letting a dog out to piss when it scratches the door. I figure they think we're worth about the same.

I grab my stuff.. shove aside a kid caught in my way. He stumbles.. grabs at me.. the smell of old cigarette smoke on his clothes when he shoves me back. I don't hesitate to throw him to the floor.. my fist in the air, ready to lay into him as he scoots away. The teacher leaps up from his desk and is between us before I get the chance, though.

He separates us.. keeps us at arm's length. —I guess I'll be seeing you again tomorrow— he says to me.

—Yeah, fine— I mumble and start to walk away. I'd have gotten detention for something else anyway, so what's the difference. All that matters now is that I'm off the hook for the rest of today.

I make my way into the hall.. pass the gym with its muffled shouting of basketball practice and whistles going off like alarms.. past the dead smell of food in the cafeteria and the echo of voices behind closed doors where different clubs are having their meetings. But soon the sound of the school fades into the sound of traffic once I pass the last few classrooms near the exit. I punch the doors open.. step into freedom and the thick shadows of taller buildings blocking out the sun.

One more day off my life.

I stopped taking the bus home a week ago. I'm in no rush to get back there. I'd rather walk.. winding my way through streets and over hills.. through crowds of tourists and businessmen and glancing over every now and again to see my reflection in the shop windows.. slumped over and mean so that people move out of my way.

There's no reason to hurry, though. Hindley gave up the show of making me do shit. He doesn't even want me around since Frances died. That's fine with me. I don't want to be around him either.. always drunk and violent. He blames me too.. says I was supposed to be taking care of her.. that somehow it's my fault she was stupid and clumsy. Doesn't matter.. as long as I stay out of sight, everything's fine. For now anyway. I'm sure I don't have long, though.. at the rate he's going crazy, I'll be out on the street for certain.. sooner or later.

I wonder if Catherine will even notice that I'm gone?

She spends all her time taking care of that baby.. Loraine. I don't know why she bothers.. it's Hindley's screaming brat. Besides, it won't do any good.. with parents like hers, she is doomed to be useless anyway.. might as well let her cry.. or die, even.

I don't mean that.

Not completely.

I just don't think Catherine should let his problems be her problems. I can't tell her, though.. she wouldn't listen to me. Even if she did, she'd just say I was being cruel. It's because they've all turned her against me.. Mrs. Linton and her fairy-tale parties.. all those plastic people telling her it's her duty to look after her family. It's all shit. Hindley's never really been her family.. never close to her the way I was. It should just be her and me.. that's all we should need to look out for.

The light in the sky has turned into the flames of early evening by the time I make it all the way back to our neighborhood. I stop for a minute to watch the way the sun touches on all the houses.. looks nothing like Heaven.. more like fire just beginning to burn things to ashes and it's almost prettier.

—Why are you standing out here?—

I turn to the side and see Isabelle standing next to me.. leaning closer and twisting her hips so that her belly button shows just below the bottom of her shirt and just above the waistband of her flower petal skirt.. pouting her lips at me as I stare at her with blank eyes.

—Leave me alone— I growl and she rolls her dumb blue eyes.

—Are you crazy or something?— giving me her silly little kid's smile that I've always hated.. hate even more today for some reason and I have to fight the urge to wipe it off her face.

I start to walk away and she skips along beside me.. leaning the right way to show off the parts of her body where her clothes are tight to her skin. There's a flash of something in her eyes then.. something about the way she looks at me and I can tell she likes me. It almost makes me smile.. knowing I could break her heart without even trying too hard at it.

—You going home?— she asks.

—Where else would I go?—

She shrugs her shoulders. —Don't know— she says. —It's just they're there— I don't need to ask who.. I know she means Edgar and Catherine and I know the thought of them annoys her as much as me when she says —They're such dorks—

When I don't respond, she starts to twist a curl of her hair around her finger.. staring at the split ends as she walks.. trying anything to get me to notice how much she's grown up the last year or so. I'm not interested. Not in her.. but as we come closer to the porch where Edgar and Catherine are tucked into each other's arms, I start to become interested in the ways Isabelle could be useful in getting back at Edgar for stealing Catherine away from me.

⊱⊰

Loraine goes down for a nap easier than ever once I get home from school. Some days it takes almost an hour to calm her down after the nanny leaves. It's exhausting having to carry her around, bouncing her and soothing her as she screams those terrible screams. But it's like she knows I needed a break today. She almost even smiles as she shakes her tiny hands good-bye when I sneak out of the room where Edgar is waiting for me in the hall.

"You're good at that," he says, nodding toward the nursery. He has the same surprised look that I always see in the movies when men watch women with babies.

I hold my finger up to my mouth, "Shhhh," smiling as I gently pull the door, leaving it open just a crack. "Anyway, it's easy."

"Not to me," he says. "I think it's amazing how you do that."

I shrug.

"Not really," I say. It's the truth too. It's not me who amazes him or any of those men in the movies. It's nature that startles them. Boys always fight against nature. Or just observe it. Girls are different. We feel nature and go along with it. But it's not something you can explain with words. Not without sounding like the crazy hippies that run all those trinket shops in the tourist part of town, talking about crystals and the flow of life energy. Besides, there's a better way to help him understand. Taking his hand in mine as I pull him down the stairs and onto the porch tells him more than any words can.

My good mood from lunch has carried over all afternoon and I just want to be outside in the sun. Be part of the world for the first time in forever, it feels like. And as soon as we get on the porch, I run to the railing. I lean forward, close my eyes, and breathe in the salty scent of the breeze blowing in from the sea. It's almost like dreaming for a moment. The way it erases any thoughts about the million and one things I have to worry about. And I try to hold on to that calm feeling when I open my eyes again. Try to make it last.

Edgar is watching me. Tracing my outline with his eyes and it makes me smile. Makes me a little shy too, because I can see how beautiful I look to him. It shows on his face. The same way he admires the design of his favorite rare cars whose beauty makes

180

them valuable. But I don't mind, because to him those cars are perfect and that means I'm perfect in his eyes too.

"What?" he asks, getting nervous by the way I'm smiling at him and I'm glad to know I can have the same effect on him that he has on me.

"Nothing," I say.

We stay standing a few feet apart. He keeps covering his mouth and rubbing his face and I keep running my hand through my hair before tucking it behind my ear. It's almost like a dance the way we both steal glances at each other while pretending not to stare. There's nothing uncomfortable or complicated about it. It's just fun every once in a while to feel like that. A feeling like being in kindergarten again.

It lasts as long as the quiet lasts.

It fades at the first screeching sound of tires in the distance.

"Oh," I say, suddenly snapping out of it. "I spoke to Nelly."

"Oh?"

"Yeah," I say. "She's okay. A little freaked out still, but fine."

Saying it freaks me out a little too. I look over at the front door, see the staircase through the glass, and a flash of memories floods in. But it's getting easier to shake them off. Easier today than yesterday. Easier tomorrow, I'm sure. Easier still if we don't talk about it.

I drag him over to the porch swing. Not that it really takes any pleading to get him to go along. He falls with me. On top of me as his hands crawl over my clothing. I slide my legs under his and my skirt slides up. His hands slip under my shirt and it's like we're dissolving into each other as soon as we start to kiss. I think it might actually happen too except that we're interrupted by his sister shouting at us from the sidewalk.

"You two are so gross," she says. "Why don't you go inside to do that?"

"Shit," Edgar mumbles as he extends his arms to push himself away from me. Then he turns his attention to her and shouts back, "Why don't you go somewhere else?"

Isabelle squints her eyes and makes the same pouting face she always uses with her mom when she doesn't get her way. She puts her hands on her hips and shuffles her weight to one foot and I don't think I'll ever get used to how much of a spoiled brat she is. "Don't have to," she says. "It's a free country." Making it impossible to believe she's actually in high school and still acts like such a child.

Edgar gives me an apologetic look. He doesn't have to bother. I don't blame him. It's not his fault she gets jealous whenever anyone pays attention to someone besides her.

"You know what, though?" she says. "I will go. Not because you said so, but because you two make me gag."

"Fine with me," he says and she storms off.

Once we're alone again, he says he's sorry. I tell him not to worry. It's not exactly like my family's perfect. His is practically the Family of the Year compared to mine. Even Isabelle's sulking is a welcome relief. At least it's normal. Not like Henry and Hindley, who both spend most of their time locked behind closed doors, planning a war against each other.

"She'll leave us alone now," he says. A playful smile creeps across his face then and he asks me if I remember where we left off.

I answer by placing my hands on the back of his neck and pulling him closer. But his prediction is a little premature. Isabelle is back after maybe ten minutes. That's not what surprises me, though. The surprise is who is with her when I look up and see Henry standing next to her.

It's a shock to Edgar too. I can tell by the way his hands tremble just before releasing me. His eyes focusing right away on how Isabelle has her elbow locked together with Henry's and how she's leaning so close to him. "What are you doing?" he asks and I'm not sure he even knows which of them he's talking to.

"None of your business," Isabelle answers, leaning even closer to Henry to show her brother that they are a couple. But I can tell he's not interested in her at all. I know he's not. It's not such a secret that he hates her. He hardly seems to notice her even now, staring right at me instead. Staring at me like I'm a criminal who he's caught in the middle of committing some terrible crime.

Edgar goes over to the steps, every inch of his body tense and ready for a confrontation. Henry notices too. He raises one eyebrow, letting a longer strand of hair fall over his eyes. But not before I catch a spark of something that tells me he enjoys getting a rise out of Edgar. One corner of his mouth curling up in a grin as Edgar's hands curl up into fists.

"Henry? What are you doing?" I ask, trying to make it sound like it's all a practical joke even though I can tell it's more serious than that. He's more serious than that. But there's a chance I can still reach him and keep things from getting out of control.

"Same thing as you," he says, linking me and Edgar with shifting eyes. So much hate in his voice that it makes my heart jump a beat when he says it. His eyes like a gun, shooting me each time he blinks. And I know that me seeing Edgar has been hard for him, but I guess I never understood just how hard until this second. Until he puts his arm around Isabelle's shoulder and brushes her cheek with his fingers. All the time staring at me with accusing eyes because he's convinced I betrayed him.

Edgar follows the movement of Henry's hand as it tickles Isabelle's skin. Makes her face turn from pale to pink. Makes her sway side to side like a kitten being petted for the first time and Edgar slowly loses control of his temper. His face turns red at a faster pace than hers as he moves off the porch and onto the first step.

"Stay away from my sister!"

The warning seems to linger over the street for an eternity. Echoing off the houses and the windows. Resting in the empty seats of the parked cars. Even the clouds act as cushions to keep Edgar's words from leaving. Keep them muffled and bouncing them back down to our lawn where Henry starts laughing.

Isabelle joins in. She loves pissing off her brother too, but for different reasons. She's just satisfied with stealing his attention back away from me. That, I understand. It's Henry who confuses me. I don't know why he has to pull her into this. Why can't he just talk to me about what's obviously bothering him? Talking used to be as simple as breathing between us.

"Are you trying to say something?" Henry says to Edgar. "Don't think I'm good enough for her?" he adds, stepping closer to a fight.

Edgar looks off down the street and shakes his head at the sky. We both know Henry is just setting him up but Edgar answers him anyway. "No, I don't. Not really," he says. "Maybe you used to be, but not anymore."

"What's that supposed to mean?"

"Means you better get your arm off of her!"

Their voices are raised for the first time. Words being spit instead of spoken. "STOP!" I shout because I'm not going to let this happen again. I'm not going to let them fight. "BOTH OF YOU! JUST STOP IT!"

I place myself between them. Wait for them to cool off enough to break eye contact, then I turn to Edgar. I put my hands on his chest and feel his blood running a million miles a second through his body. I try to make my touch calm him. Try to make my voice calm him too by whispering.

"Maybe you should go," I say.

"I'm not leaving him with her," he says quietly, but not quiet enough and I'm afraid it's going to start up again.

"Take her with you," I whisper. "I'll talk to him. I'll figure out what's going on."

After considering it long enough to let his temper fade, he nods. Says okay as long as I think I'll be okay. There's no need to worry, though. I'll be fine. It's just Henry's way to get my attention, same as Isabelle's trying to get his. Nothing more. I just need to talk to him and straighten things out, that's all.

Edgar walks up to Isabelle and tries to pull her away. She shakes him off. Shouts at him to leave her alone. Shouts for Henry to do something but Henry completely ignores her. She notices too, but pretends not to. She starts to walk away with Edgar then, but acts like she's fighting against him. Probably just to hide the embarrassment of being dismissed so easily by Henry.

I get a taste of how she feels when he brushes past me without a word. I call him back, saying his name with a sigh and telling him we need to talk. He heads right inside and doesn't even glance

185

back over his shoulder. The screen door slams shut behind him and slams again as I follow him.

}o-o{

It's getting to her..slowly..eating at her more like a snail than a lion but still it's eating at her. Catherine's jealous. Her eyes are watching my fingers stroke Isabelle's cheek and she's having a hard time hiding it.

I feel my mouth bending into a grin as Isabelle's eyelashes flutter.

It's really getting to him..getting Edgar up for a fight that I'm looking forward to. Too bad it never happens. Catherine talks him down and sends him away. He takes his sister with him. She starts begging me to help her..to stand up for her. As if I care? She served her purpose, that's all I wanted from her.

Catherine wants answers from me but I don't want to talk to her. I don't want to hear anything that comes out of a mouth that was locked onto his when I walked up. I go right past her and continue to ignore her when she follows me inside.

She follows me into the basement..asking the same question over and over as she comes down the stairs to confront me. —Why do that to her?— she asks. —Why would you pretend to like her?—

—Why would you pretend to like him?— I snap.

Catherine folds her arms in front of her and tells me that's different. —I do like him— she says. —You hate Isabelle, though. You're only trying to hurt her—

—Maybe I'm trying to hurt you!— I shout.

My words hit her like a fist and I almost regret saying them..seeing her eyes grow wider than her face can hold..seeing them grow sad..part of me wishes I could take it back, but part of me is glad she knows.

—Why?— she asks..a voice sadder than I ever heard her sound before.

I turn around so that I don't have to see her..put my hands on the table that serves as a desk and stare down at the papers strewn around..the corner of a drawing poking out under a pile..one black wing scratched out in pencil. —Because— I say. —Because you lied to me—

—I never..I— she starts to say because she can't even admit it..can't bring herself to be honest about what she's done to me.

—You did— I say..bringing myself to face her again. —You lied every time we promised never to be like them..like the Lintons..like all those people who came to Dad's funeral. But obviously you didn't mean it. You wanted to be like them all along and now you have your chance as long as you stay with him—

She tries to tell me it's not like that. —It's not like you think—

—How would you know what I think? You haven't bothered to ask me what I think— I yell. She starts to back away then..filling her eyes up with fear and future tears..and I tell her that's exactly what I mean. —You act like I'm some stranger!—

—That's not true—

—That is true! You got rid of me because I don't fit into your new perfect life with Edgar!— She reaches toward me but I shake her hand off. I don't want her to touch me. I don't want her to pity me.

—Henry? It wasn't like that— she says. —It wasn't like choosing.. it just.. happened—

I walk away.. across the room with my hands over my face.. rubbing off all the anger because I don't want to say anything more.. don't want to say what I'm thinking at this moment because it's not true.. I only feel like I hate her right now but that's because I love her too much.

—Just.. leave— I mumble.

She starts moving toward me.. says my name once.. softly like saying she's sorry but I tell her not to.. tell her again to go.

I hear her sniff louder as she says —Okay—

I wait for her footsteps to climb to the floor above.. wait for them to shuffle over the ceiling above my head before I collapse on my bed.. bury my face in the pillow, and scream so that no one can hear me.

TEN

"Shit," I say as the baby starts crying. Screaming from what used to be Henry's room. I sigh and drop my hands into my lap. I know it's wrong, but I want to ignore her. I want to be selfish just for one afternoon and pretend she doesn't exist. But the screams just get louder and I know her face is getting redder as all the air rushes out of her lungs. I pull at the ends of my hair and I know I have to get up. I can't leave Loraine like that. It's not her fault everyone else in this house has gone crazy. "Sorry, Nelly. I got to check on her."

"It's okay," Nelly says, putting her arms behind her head as she leans back on my bed.

I feel bad.

She must be so bored.

She's probably wishing I never invited her over. Taking care of Loraine is about all I've done since we came back from school. We haven't even gotten a chance to talk about anything. Not really.

Not the things we need to talk about, like what Henry said to me yesterday after that whole scene with Isabelle. I haven't been able to tell more than what actually happened. Nothing about how I feel about it, though. And Nelly hasn't had the chance to tell me how she's been dealing with everything either because every time we get past the uncomfortable silent parts, Loraine starts fussing.

I'd leave her be if I thought anyone else would go to her. Hindley won't. He won't come out of his room for anything unless it's for another drink. He just sits in there with the curtains drawn, rotting away in oblivion. He never sets foot in the nursery even if Loraine screams until the paint peels from the walls. I don't know how he can let her cry. I've never heard a sound so terrible. Like someone getting their skin burned off, that's what it sounds like when she starts crying. It seems almost impossible to me that those tiny lungs could make that much noise.

I leave my room, cross the hall into the nursery. No matter how many times I've been in here, it's still weird at first. The way the room used to smell like rain, the way Henry does, is gone. There's no trace of that scent. It has the sour smell of babies and powder now. Almost like he's been erased.

I try not to think about it.

Henry would say that's my problem. That I'm not thinking about things enough, but I disagree. I think about it plenty, but I think differently than him. I get worried when I think about me and him and about how the future between us can only get worse because Henry can only think of things in the past. He can't move on and that's what makes me think he's going to vanish from life. And that's what makes me try to hold on tighter to things that already happened. It's an endless circle where one feeds the other and I'm afraid it's going to ruin us.

I quiet Loraine by scooping her into my arms. "Shhhh. Shhhh," I whisper, moving her back and forth like the leaves moving in the wind outside the window. She's so small and helpless that it's impossible for me to be angry when I'm holding her. Her hands twisting and twitching as I walk her around the room, bouncing her on my shoulder, and tapping her on the back until the fever color fades from her skin.

Nelly's watching me from the door. Her eyebrows raised and biting her lip, staring at the baby like it's an alien or something. "She okay?"

I nod and Nelly takes a couple of careful steps closer.

"You want to hold her?" I ask.

"No way!" Nelly says. "It might puke all over me."

The horrified look on her face begins to change into a smile and when I start to laugh, she joins in. A small laugh at first but both sounds roll up into each other and before I know it, I'm laughing harder. Nelly too. It's nice. It's the first time we've felt like real friends in ages.

"I guess babies can be kind of gross," I admit.

"Kind of? C'mon! They go to the bathroom all over themselves," Nelly jokes and it sets us giggling again. Not as hard as before. Just normal kind of laughing because the tension has already been broken.

I turn at the waist so that Nelly can get a better look at the baby and it's funny how scared she looks. She's never been around babies before. But still, she gets close enough so that Loraine grabs her finger and then Nelly doesn't look so terrified anymore. Like something in the touch lets her know there's nothing to worry about.

"I guess they're kind of cute too," Nelly admits.

"Tell that to Henry," I say. "If it was up to him, he'd leave her on a doorstep somewhere."

"He doesn't like her, huh?"

"That's an understatement," I say. "He thinks I shouldn't bother with her. That she's not my problem." I look into Loraine's face, at how she stares up at me with eyes bigger than the rest of the world. "But I don't know, I sort of feel responsible for her. Like I have to be everything to her since she'll never have a mother, you know?"

"I think so," Nelly says. "But you shouldn't have to."

"I know," I say. I'm hoping Hindley will snap out of his mood once a little time has passed. Henry too. Once he isn't so mad anymore. He took care of me when I lost my mother and I know he could be just as good of a brother to Loraine too. Someday.

"How's Edgar with all of this?" Nelly asks.

"Great. As always," I say with a smile. Thinking about him always makes me smile because at least there's one good thing going on in my life.

"And how's Henry with that?" Nelly asks and I take a deep breath. Shake my head and she says that's what she thought.

"Nelly, I don't know what to do anymore." I tell her that I've tried everything I can think of, but that he won't listen to me. "I mean, I still love him. I do. And I still need him, but sometimes, it's like he's gone crazy."

"I can try talking to him," she says.

"Will you?" I ask. "Soon? I'm afraid he's going to do something."

"Like what?" Nelly asks, making it sound like I'm overreacting.

"I don't know," I say, staring out the window. "But it'll be something bad. That much I can tell."

Nelly says I'm just being nervous. "It'll be fine."

"Maybe," I say.

"Trust me, I'm sure," Nelly says and I wonder if she would be so sure about it if she'd seen the look in his eyes yesterday. If she knew that hurting my feelings actually made him happy.

I decide not to tell her, though. She'd just say I was making too much of it and he was only letting off some steam. And she'd probably be right. I'm probably not being fair to him. "Yeah, let's forget it," I say.

Loraine has fallen asleep again.

I put her down in the crib and Nelly and I head back to my room. On the way in, we make a promise to each other that for the rest of the afternoon we'll only talk about things that make us happy. I think it's a conversation both of us could use.

꙳ ꙳

I hear my name being called as soon as I turn the corner past my school. A girl's voice. It's a faint sound.. almost lost in the music of police sirens and the undertow of a million conversations passing me on the sidewalk. I don't recognize the voice so I keep walking.

It's probably a friend of the kid I fought with earlier in the day.. or yesterday maybe.. a friend of an enemy for sure and they're using her to set a trap.. get me to turn around and that's when ten of them jump out and kick me to the curb.

No such luck for them because I pretend like I never heard it.

I keep a steady pace to keep them from rushing me. I still got plenty of time to get away.. don't want to panic.. don't want them to think they can get to me. I want them to think their plan is working right up until the last second.. up until I see the bus pulling into the stop and I can get on before they can make a move.

I see the bus on the next block as the footsteps close in behind me. I stay one foot and then the other in the same rhythm as before. The timing's going to need to be perfect.

—Henry!— the girl hollers again.. desperate this time.. eager to have me look but I'm not even tempted. My hands become fists inside my pockets.. fixing my house keys between my knuckles like a weapon.. taking my hands out slowly.. carefully so that whoever is following won't catch on.. weaving in and out of people passing the other way and listening as she gains ground.

A hand presses against my back.. a touch like an electric shock and I spin around in a flash.. grabbing at her shirt.. bunching it in one hand.. my other hand held a foot away from her face. My arm bent back.. the jagged edge of my keys inches away from stabbing her through the cheek when she throws her hands over her face and screams.. saying my name again in a scared voice like she's praying and this time it sounds familiar to me.

—What the hell are you doing here?— I drop my hands back to my sides and release my grip. I push her away and she stumbles a few steps . . bumping into a person who has stopped to watch our little show.

—*God!*— Isabelle says once she's caught her balance. —Nice to see you too!— pouting her lips and fixing her hair with the stroke of her hand.

The stranger loses interest once it's obvious that we know each other and there's nothing to see . . knows that I'm not going to assault her or anything.

I lose interest too . . probably quicker than he did.

Isabelle's still fussing with her hair and straightening her blouse when I start walking away . . ignoring her plea for me to —*wait*— her hand held out toward me and I was worried something like this might happen . . that she would get the crazy idea in her mind that I actually like her and I wonder how mean I have to be to get her to stop following me.

The buildings in the distance get closer as I move toward them . . grow taller as I climb uphill where the sidewalk goes vertical for the next three blocks. Isabelle stomps her feet . . expects me to slow down for her but I have no intention of meeting any of her expectations.

—You know, I waited for you for like twenty minutes— she says . . saying it like twenty minutes is a sacrifice that I should fall on my knees and be grateful about. Whatever. I pick up my pace. She falls farther behind . . breathing heavier as the street gets steeper. —Can't you slow down for a second?— she shouts. She's nothing much more than a skeleton and can't bring herself up to my speed.

—What for? You shouldn't even be here— I slow down

long enough for her to catch up.. turn around so that we're standing face-to-face when I tell her —Just go!—

She keeps two cracks in the sidewalk between us.. flinching slightly every time I move to scratch my arm or fix my hair against the wind. —I thought we could hang out— she mumbles and all her tough attitude is gone now.

—Why?—

—Because.. that's what normal people do— she says.. putting her head down and looking at me through the top of her eyes.. making them bright and big like a doll's and twisting her curls around her finger and playing a part she thinks I want her to play.. that she thinks will make me want to sweep her up and hold her forever and ever. It's a waste of time, though, because whenever I look at her, all I see is her brother. I think about him stealing Catherine away and it's almost too easy to blame her.

—Leave me alone— I say, giving her fair warning.

—I came all the way down here— she complains. —Now you won't even hang out with me for a while?— smiling as she asks.. smiling like promising me that I won't regret going with her.

—This isn't the Heights.. this isn't anyplace you'd want to hang out— I tell her.. trying to get her to open her eyes and take a real look at this neighborhood.. at the metal gates draped over the shop windows.. at the tags graffitied on the front of each building.. at the trash nestled in the corner of each stoop. There're no cafés or parks with benches and children feeding pigeons. There're no porches to sit around on and talk about bullshit. I want her to see that she stands out like a target with her designer handbag resting easy against her pale skin. —Why don't you just get back on the bus.. or in a cab.. or whatever way you got here and go back before something happens—

—Nothing's going to happen— she says.. laughing because she doesn't know anything.. doesn't know that not every part of the city is like her safe little corner. —Besides, even if it did, I'm with you—

—You're not WITH me!— I yell.. take an aggressive step toward her. It startles her.. makes her flinch again and I wonder what the hell she wants with someone who terrifies her as much as I obviously do. I throw up my hands at how ignorant she is. —Forget it.. do what you want— I tell her —but I'm not going to look out for you—

I shove my hands deep into my pockets.. my head slumped between my shoulders as I head down a side street. Isabelle stays behind me like a shadow.. her mouth moving as fast as our footsteps.. not getting at all what I've been trying to communicate to her.. going on and on about her friends at school.. about how she told them all about me and I just shake my head.. keep my eyes on the sidewalk and let the chaotic music of the city drown her out.

Everyone always says San Francisco is so romantic.. the Paris of America.. they only say that because they don't hear the song this city really sings. It's the sound of something beautiful dying.. the last breath of an angel before the ocean swallows her.. before an earthquake breaks it off from the rest of the world and drowns it. The romance is there but it isn't what they think. Really it's the romance of saying good-bye forever.

The sun seems to agree with me.. making the towering glass buildings look like infernos as it sets on the other side of the ocean. People always seem to miss the violence in it.. only see the beauty and stay blind to what's really happening. But I guess the deception is what makes them willing to fall in love with this place, which is really nothing more than the last stop before the end of the world.

Isabelle dares to get closer to me again once it starts getting darker.. once the streetlights have flickered on and we head into the neon center of the city's strip clubs and bars.. the sidewalks crowded with drunken adults letting off clouds of cigarette smoke into the air.. the loud clatter of restaurants all around us.. the overwhelming smell of food.. people pushing this way and that like blood cells because this is the heart of the city.. everything moves out from here.. trickling into the small quiet parts.

I feel more at home in this part of the city now than in the Heights.. the electricity running through everything and making it flicker.. the speed at which the people move.. the cars and everything.. and all the noise like the hum of a mechanical ocean. It's how I feel inside lately.. all flashes of color and instinct.

—Henry?— Isabelle asks.. stepping closer to me after staying silent for so long.. close enough so she can put her hand on my elbow.. mimicking all the happy couples standing at every corner waiting for the traffic lights to change. —Why don't you like me?—

—Are you serious?— It's hard to believe even she could be so full of herself. But people like Isabelle can never understand why people like me can't stand them. They expect everyone to fall in love with them because they're rich and attractive . . because they've had everything they've ever wanted handed to them and they confuse that with thinking it makes them just as valuable as the stuff they own.

The spell doesn't work that way on me, though. I don't care about any of those things . . things that can be bought and shown off. There's only one thing I ever cared about and people just like her decided to take that too.

I hate all of them.

I hate them so much right now that I'm willing to make her pay for the rest of them . . snatching her wrists and pulling her into an alley. I can feel her bones between my fingers as I drag her away from the lights blazing out of every window. And she's so naive that she barely struggles . . thinks I'm playing a game . . that this is all so exciting. But that changes when I back her against the wall . . slamming her shoulders against the bricks and the pain makes her mouth fall open into a small circle.

—Is this what you want?— I growl at her . . squeezing her wrists harder so that they'll bruise . . so that her eyes squint up . . paying her back for every mean word that's ever been said to me by all the people she's going to grow up to be just like. —Isn't it just so much fun?— using her voice and mocking the way she talks . . the way her and her dipshit friends think it's cool to have a dangerous boyfriend.

—Stop— she says but it sounds so weak that it's easy to ignore.

I slowly raise her arms above her head . . twisting until she has to turn around and then I lean against her . . pushing my body onto hers so that she has to turn her head to keep her face from being crushed against the wall.

—You still want me to like you?— I ask. The rough brick scrapes her soft cheek. Her knees shiver and her lips start to shake and I can't help thinking how easy it would be to take her away from Edgar the same as he took Catherine away from me.

—Henry . . please— she whimpers and I barely hear her over the electric hum of the city whistling through the street a few feet away. She glances over that way but we're safe from anyone coming to her rescue. The bright lights don't shine into this hidden corner.

I let her go once the first frightened sob leaves her throat. She drops to the ground . . holding her knees close to her chest and looking up at me like a tortured pet. —Just stay away from me— I warn as she rubs the marks on her wrists and touches the scrape on her face. Her eyes stay big and blue like the sky . . like a dumb doll's. Then she holds her hand out for me to help her up because she doesn't get it.

I shake my head and go.

—Don't leave— she says . . asking me to stay with her . . calling my name but nothing else. She knows better than to follow me, though. She stays in that alley like a lost kitten meowing for someone to care. Let her find someone else.

I step back into the flood of people passing by.. becoming part of the wave and letting it drag me.. drifting until it crests and crashes.. knowing eventually I'll get washed ashore.

>< ><

It's been over two hours since Edgar called to tell me there was a problem with Isabelle and that Henry had everything to do with it. I've been pacing the whole time, waiting for him to call back. Moving from the windows on the far side of my room to where the bookcases are, pausing to stare at the titles for the hundredth time before I turn around. Then when I make my way back to the window, I glance out at the street for a second. After that, I do it all over again, wearing a path through the floor and wearing out Nelly as she tries to follow me with her eyes.

My hands are just as nervous as my feet. I keep tapping them against my leg, against my chin, and against the spine of every book lined up on the shelves. It's like my fingers are trying to keep up with the thoughts racing through my mind. So many, like cars on the freeway. Speeding by too fast to focus. Passing each other one after the other. I keep pacing, hoping I can slow them down and get them lined up in a way that makes sense.

"Seriously, Catherine, you need to stop," Nelly says. "You're making me dizzy."

I stop long enough to say I'm sorry. Then I go back to marching from one end of the room to the other. Nelly's used to me being neurotic, though. She deals with it by sighing and leaning back on the bed, but her eyes continue their marathon. Back and forth. Bouncing from one side to the other.

"I'm really sorry," I tell her. I've put her through enough drama lately. "I never wanted to be one of those girls whose life is like a soap opera."

"It's okay," she says. But the way she says it shows that she's a little bit annoyed. "It's not your fault," she says in a softer tone.

"I know, but still . . ." And I'm afraid if I apologize once more she's going to scream so I just let my voice trail off from there. Let my hands travel over the wallpaper. Dragging them behind me until I reach the bookshelves again where I can read the titles with my fingertips like blind people. "It still feels like it is, though, you know?"

"You need to stop worrying," she says. "Everything's going to be fine, you'll see."

"Yeah," I say, even though I don't really believe it.

I start to pace faster when the voices downstairs get louder. Nearly screaming. Mrs. Linton's voice mostly. Finding its way up to my room in angry pieces. Hysterical outbursts that don't last long enough to make sense of, like shooting stars that burn for an instant then fade out once you blink.

"What do you think they're going to do?" Nelly asks.

I shrug and tell her I'm trying not to think about it.

"Will they call the police, you think?"

I shake my head, but it's more of a wish. There's no telling what Hindley will do to get his hands on Henry if he doesn't show up soon. He'll have him hunted down if he has to. Mrs. Linton's not like that. She's not mean the way Hindley is when he's drunk. But she's so upset about Isabelle that she might turn that way.

I start biting my nails as I pace, praying that Isabelle is fine. For Henry's sake, I hope she is.

Mrs. Linton will calm down once she knows everything is all right. Once Edgar gets back here and she can see that Isabelle was probably exaggerating. This should all blow over then.

"How did this happen again?" Nelly asks.

"I'm not sure," I mumble, taking my hand away from my mouth. "All I know is what Edgar told me. Isabelle called him and said Henry attacked her. Said she was downtown and that he was going to get her."

"Why was Henry even with Isabelle?" Nelly asks, trying to figure it out in her head. "Didn't you say he was just fooling around with her yesterday? Why would he bother with her again?"

"I think that's what they're trying to figure out," I say.

I have an idea but I haven't told her. It's too hard to explain that he would be with her just so he could do something like this. She wouldn't believe me. She wouldn't understand about the way Henry's eyes used to have something bright behind the blackness like the night sky, all dark at first glance until the stars came out. Lately, there haven't been any stars. His eyes stay dark all the time. I don't know how to tell her that without sounding like I'm the one who's crazy.

I'm not, though. I know the truth. There's something mean about him now. I've seen it even if I don't want to admit it. I saw it when I told him about Frances that night. I saw it the other day too when Loraine was screaming. I rushed into the living room where she was and Henry was just sitting there listening to her cry. Just listening. And I know for certain that I saw it yesterday, the way he was enjoying it when I got upset.

It's like there's no room in his heart for any feeling other than hate.

It's hard for me to believe it. It's hard for me to imagine the same boy who used to pick bouquets of dandelions for me could ever be so cruel.

We both hear Hindley charging up the stairs. Stopping on the second floor to yell, "Catherine!" His voice thundering through the walls. "Catherine, get down here!"

I'm already down to the third floor by the time he finishes saying it. I lean over the railing. I can see his eyes are red and glassy. Burning eyes. I don't want to come any nearer, so I stay a floor above him. Nelly stays a floor above me, her arms nervously folded across her chest as she watches.

"Where is he?" Hindley demands. Letting his anger out on me. Letting it out anywhere he can because this house is infected with it. Woven into the carpets. Slowly eating away at every board and nail that holds it together. Anger is all that's left of Hindley too when he starts raging at anything and everything, expecting it to give in to him. "Tell me where he is!" he yells.

I feel it getting inside me too.

I feel my body mirroring his. The corners of my mouth curling around my teeth and opening wider to let my words shoot out like fire. "How am I supposed to know?" I yell.

"He tells you everything, that's how!"

"Not anymore, thanks to you!" I shout. "You've done everything you could to drive us apart!"

"Not everything, but I will now," he says, growling through clenched teeth. He starts nodding slowly as a smile creeps across his face like a threat. The way he did when we were kids. The way

he does whenever he's about to say something meant only to be hurtful. "He's gone. When he walks through that door, it'll be the last time. I don't want him around this house or this family. I've got enough to deal with."

"Enough to deal with? You don't deal with anything!" I scream. My fingers wrap around the staircase railing, gripping it so tightly it shakes. "Your answer to every problem is just to lock it away. You locked Henry away in the basement. You leave Loraine for other people to take care of. You even lock yourself away in your room. YOU. DON'T. DEAL. WITH. ANYTHING!"

He rushes at me two steps at a time.

I don't flinch or back away.

I stand up straight and wait for his hand to slap me. And when he does, his palm touches my face like a fever. A sudden shattering sound in the air as the force of the blow pushes my body against the banister.

When I rub the sore spot on my cheek, Nelly cups her hand over her mouth to hold in the last fragments of a scream. I run my tongue over my teeth to taste for bleeding. There is none and I look up at Hindley standing over me.

I want to hurt him.

I want to find the right words that will get to him. And when I do, I let them slip out of my mouth like a poison. "You can be as mean to us as you want," I mutter, "but you'll always be Dad's least favorite."

Hindley raises his hand above his head, breathing heavily to gather up enough drunken strength to strike me harder than last time.

Mrs. Linton scrambles up the stairs before he can. "Stop it!"

she yells, trembling as she reaches our floor. Her makeup streaked down her face like sidewalk paintings washed away in the rain. Her arms shaking when she pushes Hindley away from me. "Stop it," she says again, but this time it's not as forceful. Not like someone fighting. More like the sound of someone giving up.

I'm ready to give up too.

He's won.

He's finally finished what he came back here from L.A. to do. He's destroyed any trace of Heaven left in this house and turned every warm feeling to dust. The truth of it is written across my face with his handprint. I'll never forgive him for it.

Everyone else feels it at the same time too. They sense it the same way as me. That anything good that ever lived in this place has been stamped out. Even Loraine can tell and instinctively she starts crying.

"I'll get her," Nelly says. She quickly retreats and I see the relieved expression on her face. Happy for any distraction that will let her escape.

Mrs. Linton glares at Hindley as she helps me to my feet. Her disapproval doesn't register through his faded eyes, though. His face still flush with anger. Still lost in it as the front door opens and he springs to life.

"If that's him, I'll kill him," he roars, making a break for the stairs. Mrs. Linton reaches for him but he's charging away too fast. I go after him then. Stumbling three steps at a time and around the landing to the next set of stairs. Screaming at him to stop. Screaming because I can't catch up.

By the time he realizes that it's Edgar, it's too late to slow down.

They collide.

Hindley falls like a tornado running out of wind.

I see Isabelle step back onto the porch. She waits for the commotion to cool down before coming inside again. The chandelier shining on her like a spotlight and I study her like looking for cracks in a glass that's been dropped.

"Isabelle?" Mrs. Linton brushes by me. Gathers Isabelle in her arms like mothers do with toddlers in the park after they tumble onto the pavement.

"I'm fine!" Isabelle snaps, wiggling out of her mother's arms like a snake slithering off a branch. Steps away. Rolling her eyes at all the attention. "It was nothing."

"Nothing? You were assaulted?" Mrs. Linton says, her voice growing impatient the way it sometimes gets when I'm over at their house and Isabelle is giving her a hard time. She starts to check for any injuries. Placing her hands on Isabelle's cheeks and turning her head from side to side.

"Mom, she's fine," Edgar says in a calm voice that slowly brings the panic to a stop. He glances quickly up at me as he finishes speaking. A blue spark of electricity in his eyes telling me that there's more to it than he's letting on but he's keeping it quiet until we're alone.

Hindley approaches Isabelle. Mumbling questions at her that she ignores. His whispers growing mean and violent until Mrs. Linton pulls her daughter away. A flash in her expression like a memory of how he slapped me and she tells him, "Come on, we're going," she says, leading Isabelle away with both hands firmly placed on her shoulders.

Hindley turns to me. He sees my fingers in my mouth and that my whole body is shaking. "This isn't over," he says to me, slurring his words from exhaustion and too many sips of whiskey. "I won't let him destroy this family's name by acting like some maniac out there on the streets!"

Edgar moves toward him. "Hey. Calm down, okay?" he says, trying to reason with a madman, but Hindley swings his arm at him like shooing an insect. He would have hit him too, if he wasn't distracted. If there wasn't a more desirable target entering through the back door.

We both know it's Henry and with one look, Hindley warns me to stay out of his way as he heads for the kitchen.

I hurry over to Edgar. Hide my face in the collar of his jacket. Digging my fingernails into him to keep from screaming when I hear the first sounds of breaking glass in the other room.

"What's going on?"

I look up and see Nelly leaning over the railing. She hurries down the stairs and points toward the back of the house where Hindley's and Henry's voices continue to shout. She stares blankly at me and Edgar. Accusingly. Wondering how we can just stand here and listen. Then she narrows her eyes, letting us both know she's not willing to.

"Don't go in there! Please," I beg.

"What's wrong with you? You act like he's not even our friend anymore!" she yells. She doesn't know that the sound she hears is years of hatred finally finding a way out. No one is safe coming between that. Luckily the back door opens and slams shut before she makes it into the room. I know that sound means Henry took off. It's become a familiar noise. Another note in the song sung in this house over the past few months.

"Don't come near here again!" Hindley shouts.

He's answered by swears that fade away from the house.

Nelly turns for the front door. "You can give up if you want, but I'm going to talk to him," she says. Running out the door before I even get the chance to talk her out of it or tell her I'm coming with her.

I wrap my arms around Edgar. Holding so tight because I feel myself being torn in two. Half of me wants to fly away after them and the other half wants to stay here where Edgar's hands stroke my hair.

I give in to the warm touch of his fingers behind my ears. The soothing sound of his voice telling me it's going to be okay. "Everything will be okay, Cat." I give in because for a moment, all I want to do is pretend that I believe him.

ELEVEN

Henry.. be reasonable— Nelly says.. banging her hands against her knees as she sits on the beach with her legs folded under her.. her eyes almost invisible in the moonlight that reflects off the sand.

—I'm never reasonable. Just ask Catherine— smirking up at the stars as I say it.. remembering how Catherine would get so frustrated with me sometimes as she tried to explain certain ways she has of understanding the world and I'd stare at her with a vacant expression. She'd tell me it was perfectly reasonable and say I was doomed to be a Pisces forever.. that I'd always be lost at sea.

—This isn't funny— Nelly scolds.

—I realize that— I say.

—Then why won't you go back there and apologize?— she asks, but the idea never takes root.. carried off by the wind as soon as it leaves her mouth.. blown into the distance like the sand she wipes from her eyes when it's kicked up during a gust. —Tell them you're sorry and that you'll make up for it—

—Make up for what? I didn't do anything!— I shout .. leaning toward her .. close enough to startle her because she's like the rest of them. Sure, she came out here acting like she's trying to help me .. but it's only so she can convince herself that she's somehow better .. that she's not judging me.

It's a lie, though.

I'm nothing more than a charity case for her .. a pet project to prove how good and nice she is. She lets the truth break through when she looks at me .. the same way she'd look at any of the jerks that stroll through the hallways of my school. Well, piss on that! I'm not going to play along.

It doesn't stop her from playing, though .. trying to be the good friend, but I see right through it.

—What do you mean you didn't do anything?— she says. —What about Isabelle?— raising her eyebrows in accusation .. frustrated at my lack of cooperation. —Why would you even do that?—

—Do what?— I bark.

—Gee! I don't know? Attack her— she says .. getting up on her feet to face me .. to stand up to me .. trying to convince me that I'm wrong.

—Come off it. Don't act like you care what happens to her— I'm sick of people being so righteous around me .. so quick to tell me what I need to do differently without taking a look at themselves for even a quick glance. —You talk crap about her all the time .. but I'm supposed to be nice to her?—

—That's not the point!— she shouts..shoving me backward into the sand.

—You don't get it, do you?— I say. —I'm not sorry. I should've done worse. I should've beat some color into her pale face!— Picturing it as I say it.. my fist making contact with Isabelle's skin.. the crack of her bones like the snapping of branches in the wind. —Maybe then things would be even!—

My words echo off the rocks behind us.. repeating the last syllables before being dampened by the sand and swallowed up by the Pacific.

Nelly waits before she speaks.. catching me in her soft eyes.. with her calm voice. —Get even with who, Henry?— she asks.. a different expression on her face this time.. more afraid of what I mean rather than how I look.

—Even with everyone— I mumble. —All of them—

I know it comes out sounding crazy as soon as the words escape me. I guess I've thought about getting revenge for so long that I've convinced myself that it makes sense. But it sounds different out in the open than it did in my mind. Suddenly it all feels so stupid. It's not really what I want.. I don't really care about getting even so much. It's just been a way to keep my mind off what's really bothering me.

Nelly knows it too. Maybe she even knows better than I do that this is really all about me losing Catherine. She sits down beside me.. touches my arm and tells me —She still cares about you, you know— doing her best to make it sound like it's enough as she presses her cheek to my shoulder and stares out at the tide creeping toward our feet.

—It's not the same thing—

—Maybe not— Nelly says. —But that doesn't mean you should throw away the rest of your life—

—What life? What do I have? My life isn't like yours anymore in case you didn't notice. There's no chance of college, career, or any of that— I tell her. —I have nothing. I never had anything before her and now I've lost even that—

—You haven't lost her— Nelly says. —It's just.. different, that's all—

I shake my head. —No.. I have— I say, keeping my eyes on her eyes. —But maybe.. I mean if I can get her alone.. maybe I could get her back— saying it to myself as much as to Nelly because I can't give up without trying one last time to make Catherine remember what we learned the first time we saw each other.. that we're meant for each other.

Nelly wraps my hand in both of hers to let me know she's on my side. —Just.. don't do anything stupid, okay?—

I take a deep breath and nod. —Can you tell her? Let her know I'm coming to see her later?— I ask.

She's slow to promise but eventually she does.. eventually she says —okay— before standing up and taking a few slow steps away.. facing me with folded hands in the shape of prayer as she leaves. I watch until she fades into the night.. until she becomes part of the city in the background.. disappearing among the lights that crawl like electric fireflies through the skyline.

Once I'm alone, I surrender to the pull of the tide.. letting myself drift.. hoping that when I finally come to rest, it will be in a familiar place.. a place where there's me and

Catherine and everything else becomes scenery as soon as our eyes meet.

⊁⊰

I've seen him stand in my doorway like this so many times that it shouldn't seem strange. But it does. Even though everything about the way he leans to the side and holds the door frame like it's something delicate is the same as always, it still seems different this time. Like something's not right or out of place.

Maybe it's just been too long.

Time has a way of changing things in my mind. Everything becomes the way I picture it in my memory instead of how it really is. It was like that with my mother. I used to replay the memories I had of her over and over like watching the same movies a thousand times until I knew every little way she moved. Her image so familiar that it was burned on the back of my eyelids. But a year ago, I found some pictures of the two of us and the woman in them didn't look like her. Not the way I'd made her look in my memory anyway.

It's the same now with Henry.

The image of him in my mind feels more real than he does standing in front of me. Feels closer to my heart. That's not really his fault. It's my mistake, but that doesn't change the way it feels inside. Doesn't change the fact that he feels a little bit like a stranger when I ask him in.

"Did Nelly tell you I was coming?" he asks.

"Yeah," I say in a faint whisper.

He walks across my room. Retracing the steps from the hall to

215

the corner of my bed that he's traveled a million times before, but there's something nervous in the way he walks. His hands in his pockets. Keeping his head down and never once looking me in the eye. Acting like this is the first time he's ever been in here.

"It's okay that I came, right?" he says.

I bite my lip and nod.

I'm not sure it's the truth. Not yet. I didn't know what to say when Nelly called me. I stayed quiet when she said Henry was coming to see me. Even held my breath. Then she told me he wasn't doing well. "You need to see him," she said.

I agreed because I was afraid of what he might do if I didn't.

I asked Edgar to go. He didn't want to leave, but I pretended to be tired. I promised to see him in the morning. I didn't tell him about Henry. I knew he'd never leave if I did.

I watched him from my window after he left. Caught him staring back at me and I wanted to call him back. But I owe Henry at least until morning. I owe him a chance to give me his side of the story.

"I'm leaving," Henry says. He's not really talking to me. He's speaking to his own reflection hovering like a ghost in the window. His eyes are far away like he's already left. Part of him anyway and the rest of what's left is just trying to catch up.

I know what he's going to ask before it happens. I can sense it the way I've always been able to sense what he's thinking. Like our fates were knotted together before we were born and have never been able to separate. We've always been connected that way and that's why it's not a surprise when the words come out of his mouth.

"Will you come with me?" he asks.

I walk over and stand next to him. So close that our bodies are nearly touching. So close that I can almost feel how scared he is. I can feel his heart beating like a rabbit inside his chest when I rest my hands on his rib cage. All my memories of him come flooding back to me in a sudden spark like stars exploding. All the things I love about him eclipsing all the things that have driven us apart recently.

"Where are you going?" I ask him.

"Does it matter?"

Our eyes meeting for the first time. Mine like the sky during the day and his like the sky at midnight. And it doesn't matter then. Wherever he goes, I need to go with him. Because he would for me. He'd follow me wherever I asked him to. It's the way it's always been with us. Like a promise too important for me to break.

"Okay, I'll go," I say. If there's still a chance to bring him back to the way he was, I have to try.

Henry tries to slide his arms around my waist but I pull away. Carefully. Making it look like a misunderstanding because I'm not going with him for the reason he thinks. But I can't let him know that. If he suspects I'm going to try and talk him into staying here, he'll run off by himself and I'll never see him again.

"Come on," he says. "Let's go before Hindley hears us."

He hurries me along. Taking my hand and leading me into the hallway, where I can hear Loraine starting to fuss and I hesitate. Henry looks at me, then at the nursery that used to be his room. His eyes growing darker in the shadows as they warn me off. Telling me to leave her. That she's not mine. Saying it all with a glance and that's all it takes because the connection between us is stronger when our hands are tangled up into one.

I almost forgot how his hand felt in mine.

How everything he feels is written in his fingerprints, passing through him and into me like electricity running between us. And slowly his thoughts drown out my own thoughts as he pulls me down the stairs and through the back door. One thought louder than the others. The one that tells me he loves me.

He's in love with me and has been forever. It's so clear. So easy to tell now that I'm not trying so hard to figure it out.

I love him too. It's just not the same way and I wonder if he can tell that. If my hands speak to him the way his are speaking to me.

We cut through the backyard and make our way along the cliffs leading into the park. It's our old walk. The path we took together to and from school for ten years. And it's almost like time traveling when we leave the houses behind because we are in our own private world again. Only I feel less at home than I used to. Feel more like a visitor in an old place that isn't the same as the last time I was here.

"Remember how we used to pretend this was our home? Like we were the last two people on earth?" Henry says. I nod but he can't see me because he's facing forward and the fog is starting to roll in. "You remember?" he asks and this time I tell him verbally that I do.

"I remember," I say and even though I can't see his face either, his hands are still telling me everything and I know he's smiling.

"We'd run around for hours until we were out of breath. Then we'd fall down and just lie there in the dirt," he says, telling a story that I've lived a thousand times.

He doesn't tell me the next part but he knows I'm thinking about it the same as he is. Remembering how we'd let our fingers crawl over each other like spiders. Giggling whenever the spiders would sneak under each other's clothing and tickle our skin. The first time we played that game was the first time I told myself I was going to marry him.

But we're not kids anymore and I don't want to play.

The wind starts blowing and Henry picks up the pace. He tugs harder on my arm. Pulling me quicker through the fog the way he used to when he was trying to convince me there was nothing lurking in the mist waiting to snatch me away. And just like then, he ignores my reluctant attempts to slow him down. Goes faster instead. Pulling me closer to the blinking lights of the bridge that barely shine through the clouds that have dropped out of the sky.

The dirt beneath our feet turns to concrete as we step onto the bridge.

The rustling of the leaves turns into the hum of traffic roaring a few feet away. A swarm of headlights to greet us. A stampede of cars that makes the walkway vibrate under us. The wind coming off the ocean grows stronger too. Moving me side to side as the pulse of traffic moves me up and down. And Henry pulling me forward until there's too much and I finally break away to stand my ground.

"Henry? What's this all about?" I ask, getting up the courage to stop pretending and deal with what's really going on. "Why are you doing this?"

"Doing what?" The tone of his voice has changed. It loses the soft sound of the waves that pass hundreds of feet below and borrows the angry sound of the car engines. "What is it that I'm doing?"

I've heard him sound like this before, but never with me.

It startles me enough to take a step away from him. And I think that startles him. I can see him struggling to stay calm as he grabs hold of the railing with both hands and leans forward far enough to stare into the ocean. Suddenly he looks so small. So sad and I know that he needs my help.

The lights on the walkway make the fog glow as I approach him. Makes Henry look like he's wearing a halo around him. Erases his dark mood when he looks at me again. And when I hold my hand toward him, his eyes are still black like midnight but like a midnight under a full moon.

"Henry, come home with me?" I ask, hoping to get through to him even if for only a moment.

"Why?" he mutters. "It's not my home. Not anymore." There's something sad about the way he sounds then. Shaking his head like he's given up on everything.

"I understand it's hard right now," I tell him. "Things are crazy. But they won't always be like this. You know that! Just come back and it'll all work out."

Henry almost laughs.

He starts shaking his head again. Quicker than before, like he's wiping away the things I've said. "Don't tell me that," he says. "You know that's not true." His eyes accusing me of lying, of trying to trick him, and it's my turn to get angry with him, raising my voice to the roar of traffic.

"No! I don't know that!" I shout. "That's the whole point! We don't know anything for sure."

"I do!" he shouts, turning toward me with wide eyes that are less like moonlight now and more like the fire in shooting stars. "I know if I go back there, Hindley's just going to kick me out. I'll end up in some group home getting my ass kicked every time I give someone a wrong look, just like at Bayside! Tell me I'm not right!

Go on! Lie to me and tell me it'll all be the same as it was before if I go back there!"

His words are absorbed by the fog as I stand there, silently biting my lip and trying to hide the sadness from showing in my eyes. Because even though he doesn't say it, I can tell he blames me for everything.

When he finally speaks, he's talking to the ocean instead of me. Facing the emptiness in front of him, his back turned on the city lights that twinkle in the haze behind us. "You asked me once if I ever thought about what it would be like to be one of the birds flying over this bridge," he says and I hold my breath. Worried that he's going to show me what it's like by spreading his arms and letting his body swoop down to the water's surface. "I said it wouldn't be much different, you remember?" I bite my lip harder and nod to let him know I haven't forgotten. "I was wrong," he says. "It would be a lot different. It would be better."

"How?" I ask. "How would dying be better?"

"I'm not talking about dying," he says. "I'm talking about being free. Like birds. Just going wherever we want. This is our chance to see what it's like," he says. "We can get out of here. Just me and you like we always dreamed about."

I don't have the words to tell him that those dreams are not mine anymore. My mouth won't make the sounds because I won't let it. Not when I see that it's the old Henry who's waiting for me to either go with him or leave him behind. The same Henry who used to be so gentle. It's him again. And I know that I can save him now.

"Okay," I tell him, forcing myself to smile. "Where are we flying to?"

Henry smiles at me for the first time in forever.

"I'll show you," he promises and I decide to trust him. Following him through the clouds like running through Heaven. And I start to believe I could fall in love with him again once we get to the other side.

※ ※

The connection between us is broken when Catherine's hand slips out of mine. It's more than her touch that leaves me . . it's all of her . . like she's becoming a ghost and won't be able to understand me much longer.

—Henry . . what's this all about?— she says . . stomping her foot against the vibration of the bridge before forcing her body into an angry stance like we're fighting. —Why are you doing this?— she demands, sounding like a hostage being taken against her will.

I ask her what it is she thinks I'm doing . . asking her in an angry voice because she's acting like she's been doing me a favor up until now . . like if I ask her to go one more step, I'll be asking too much.

Then there's that look in her eyes again like she's afraid of me.

I have to stop snapping at her like that.

I need to control myself.

I place my hands on the cold steel of the bridge and lean over . . let everything mean and ugly that's inside me fall far below into the water and breathe in the easy sway of the waves. I can feel my thoughts shifting tides . . remembering now why I brought her here . . remembering that it will take time but knowing that as long as we're alone she'll come back to me.

It's slowly starting to work.

She moves closer to me . . places her hand on my back . . her fingers walking like little spiders over my shoulder blades. —Henry— she says —come home with me?— The way she asks me makes it sound like I'm being irrational . . like someone asking a little kid to stop throwing a tantrum.

—Why? It's not my home . . not anymore— I tell her. My mind is already made up about that. I don't care what her friends have told her. I know they say I'm overreacting and being dramatic . . that I'm just out for attention, but those clichés don't apply to my situation. They don't take into account a drunken tyrant with a lifetime of hatred for me.

—I understand . . it's hard right now . . things are crazy— she tells me . . talking down to me even if she doesn't mean to. —But they won't always be like this . . you know that! Just come back and it'll all work out—

Could she really understand so little about what's going on? Could she really have missed it all . . so lost in her new life that she doesn't see how things will never be the same if we go back there?

—Don't tell me that . . you know that's not true— I say.

—No! I don't know that!— She's the one shouting now because she actually thinks she needs to help *me* understand . . that I'm the one who can't see reality . . telling me that we can't ever really *know* anything for certain.

I tell her that I do.

I know Hindley will ship me off as soon as he can because he's got no use for me.

—Tell me I'm not right— I shout.. daring her to stop and really see the truth of what's happened in that house over the last few months. —Go on! Lie to me and tell me it'll all be the same as it was before if I go back there!— yelling at her louder.. angrier than before. And I'm dreading the look creeping up in her eyes, but somehow I have to make her see that she hasn't faced up to what's going on. I'm spelling it all out for her because she needs to understand that I'm not going to let him control what happens to me anymore.. I'd rather run away than let him determine my fate. So I yell.. hoping she'll agree with me if I say it all loud enough.

But my words die off in the fog.

The constant hum of tires driving over the concrete takes over again.

I can tell she still doesn't understand so I try to make her see it in a different way. I ask if she remembers when we talked about the birds and what it would be like to fly above the ground. I told her I didn't think it would be much different, but I was wrong. —It would be a lot different— I tell her now. —It would be better—

At first she thinks I'm talking about suicide.. about taking a dive off the Golden Gate, letting my body wash up on Alcatraz and learning to fly that way. But that's not what I mean at all and it worries me that we're losing the ability to communicate.. having to tiptoe around our words when we used to be able to know each other's thoughts with a simple glance.

—I'm talking about being free..like birds..just going wherever we want— I explain to her..telling her that this is our chance to find out..to run and run and run until we leave everything else behind us..so far away that our problems can't catch up. It's a dream we used to share..whispering it to each other so many times while we watched the sun sinking into the ocean.

It can be like that on the other side of the bridge.

It can be like crossing into Heaven as long as she comes with me.

I try one last time to tell her with my eyes..stealing light from the street lamps that illuminate the walkway..borrowing brightness from the headlights slicing through the fog..from the fuzzy electric glow of the city hidden in the distance and the stars hiding in the opposite direction. I steal it all and rearrange the light to make images flash against my eyes..like a movie flickering at fast speeds..home movies of us in the past..promises of what we can have in the future if we trust each other the way we were always meant to. The images pass from my eyes to her eyes on the wind..play against the backdrop of the fog like a projector screen, and I can see her tongue pushing on the inside part of her mouth the way it does when she's considering something very seriously.

I focus harder..letting her see the way that I see her.. letting her know that she's the only beautiful thing I've ever known.

It seems like forever passes before I can breathe again..
before I hear her voice saying —okay— only one word in
millions that she's ever said to me but it's the most important one.

—Where are we flying to?— she asks then and suddenly it
feels like it did when we were children.. making the games
we played seem real by believing in them so hard that the real
world got erased. That's how it feels when I smile at her.

—I'll show you— I say.. spreading my arms like feather-
less wings as I glide across the bridge.. racing the cars.. running so fast to keep anything from touching us and making it
all disappear because our world is still fragile and any crack
could crumble it. We have to get to the other side to make it
stable.. to shut out all those people and things that destroyed it before.

On the other side of the bridge, there's a national park
that stretches out for miles and miles.. empty of everything
but what we imagine.. of everyone except us if we're careful. We'll be able to live forever in there.. nothing to care
about except for being together.

I get across first, steering us off the path and onto the
rocks.. picking a trail through the pines that seem even
taller than the buildings downtown. I keep running until
my lungs burn with the damp air.. run until we've outraced
the city and I wait for Catherine to catch up.. watching her
appear through the fog like an angel.

—It's beautiful here— she says.. pausing to catch her
breath but never letting her glance rest in one spot. She looks at
the branches hanging above us like the crisscrossing electric

wires that move the buses through the streets . . stares at the way the fog moves through the trees like steam rising from grates in the sidewalk. In the city those things happen because somebody makes them happen. It happens on its own out here . . happens like magic. It's the way she has always told me she imagines Heaven to be. I needed to show her . . to bring her here so she'd remember.

—We can stay as long as we want— I tell her. —Then from here . . we can go anywhere— I rattle off a hundred possible futures for us . . images of us in New York and the North Pole . . on tropical islands or in the desert . . my eyes opening wider each time our world expands in my imagination . . speaking faster and faster, trying to make the rest of our lives happen all at once. —There's nothing to stop us— I tell her. —We can always be together from now on—

Catherine looks over her shoulder . . looking back the way we came and I can tell she doesn't really want to leave everything behind.

—What is it? What's wrong?— I ask her . . reaching for her hand and trying to reassure her that this is the way things are supposed to be . . this is our fate.

—It's just . . it's really late . . and I think we should go— saying it through her fingers to soften the blow . . saying it almost in a whisper because she knows it's not what I want her to say because this was all a trick . . coming with me. She never believed what I was saying . . it was just a way to stall until she could convince me to change my mind.

—Unbelievable— I mumble . . shaking my head at her.

—What?— she asks . . taking both of my hands in hers

and playing nice with her eyes..making herself smile as she says —Come on. Let's go back home?—

I squeeze her hands harder..so hard that she tries to pull them away because it's hurting her. It shows on her face, but I can't let go. I need to press harder..grab her by the wrists and force her to look at me..to stare me in the eyes and hear me. —There's nothing for us to go back to!—

She doesn't answer me with words. She says it with her expression..says it with every inch of her squirming, trying to get away. —Nothing for you— That's what her eyes tell me. I'm the one who's alone, she has something to go back for..she doesn't want to stay with me.

—It's him, isn't it?— I ask and she pretends not to know what I'm talking about. —It's Edgar, isn't it?— and I start shaking her to get an answer..to get her to admit it once and for all.

—No— she says..twisting her hips and struggling with her arms. But I'm stronger and I'm not letting go..not until she tells me the truth. —I mean..it's not just him— she says in a quieter voice.

It takes a second before it sinks in..before I let my hands release her. It takes even longer for me to be able to look at her again. And when I do, I can tell she's never taken her eyes off of me..feeling sorry for me..staring at me like I'm some puppy tossed into the streets. Then she comes closer to me, all full of sympathy..holding out her arms to comfort me, but I shrug her off.

—Do you love him?— I ask.

She doesn't even have the guts to answer me..only nods.

Her eyes filling up and getting pink around the edges like she's the one with a broken heart. —Henry?— she says. —I still love you.. just not the same way—

Every muscle in my body is twisted so tight it feels like they might snap from my bones when I confront her.. when I place my hands on her sides and shake her.. screaming—*You're right.. it's not the same way!*— because nothing she feels for Edgar can ever compare with what we have.

She doesn't try to pull away like I expect.. she places her hands on my neck instead.. tilts my head toward her and shows me that she's not afraid. —You're my best friend, Henry— she says —You'll always be my best friend—

—No— I tell her —you're wrong.. we'll never be friends!—

I pull her body into mine before she can respond.. put my mouth over hers to swallow any reason she might come up with to tell me I'm wrong because I know when we kiss, she'll see that we're meant to be together. I just have to hold her until she figures it out.. keep my tongue pressed to hers long enough that my words become her words.. even when she tries to pull away, I have to pull her back and never let her go.

It's the only way.. my only chance to get to Heaven.

TWELVE

There're no shooting stars. No unicorns running on rainbows or pink hearts floating like bubbles up through the clouds. No fireworks exploding in pretty colors either. There's none of that when Henry kisses me. There's only the whisper of the wind through pine trees. The damp feel of fog against my skin. The world is exactly the same as it was the moment before our lips touched.

I've imagined kissing him so many times in my daydreams. And every time, that's how I pictured it.

Me.

Henry.

All the pretty things a girl can think of all swirling around us in the sky.

That's the way I knew it would be. It was something I knew as clearly as my own name. Even as I got older, I still believed. Not so much in the unicorns or heart-shaped bubbles, not physically anyway, but the idea was real. The feeling would feel like those things.

But when he kisses me now, I feel it only with my senses.

I feel his mouth pressed against mine.

I feel his tongue fighting mine.

I don't feel any emotion at all except maybe being sad because all the magical things have gone away.

I pull away but he pulls me closer. Kisses me more when I try to kiss him less. It's like he knows what I want to say. That I want to tell him to stop. And so he's eating my words before I get the chance. But he has to feel it too. He has to be able to tell that this is the way we're finding out we aren't meant to be together.

"Stop," I manage to get out before he covers my mouth a second time and then a third until I have to fight him to even breathe. "Listen to me," struggling to get the phrase out but it's no use.

He's somewhere else.

He's someone else too and I have to get away if he's ever going to be himself again. Because I am a poison to him. Every mistake he's made lately is because of me. I'm ruining his life by being here, not saving it.

He'll only get better by getting over me and that's why I have to go. That's why I have to do it when I push him away. Kicking to overpower him and breaking for the woods at the first chance.

He'll follow me.

I'll have to be faster for his sake.

He'll know that someday. That I'm running for him and not away from him and maybe then he won't hate me for it. Maybe then we can be friends. Maybe then he'll love me the way I love him.

✄ ✄

She's ahead of me. Too far for me to see through the fog.

I can hear her, though..her sneakers striking the ground..a steady rhythm that is slower than mine and I know I can catch up with her.

I have to.

I have to finish explaining things to her if she'll listen.

It's so clear to me now what went wrong between us. It all made sense the moment we kissed. I felt like myself for the first time since before Mr. Earnshaw died. Since then I've been trying to be somebody else..ever since Hindley told me to stay away from her. I can't be me when I'm away from her. I'm nobody then..but as long as we're together I'll always be the person she loves.

Those are the things I need to tell her.

Those are the magic words that will bring our world to life again.

—Catherine..wait—I shout..letting her know I'm near.. that I'm coming. But she doesn't wait..doesn't slow down.

I hear her turn off the path..the sound of her feet trampling through leaves and grass..snapping twigs and kicking at stones.

I stop running..let my hands fall to my knees and collect my breath.

—I'm sorry— I shout. I never should have kissed her like that..it's never how I meant it to be but there was no other choice. It was the only way to figure things out. It's like the fairy tales she used to read to me when I first came to live there. I needed her to kiss me before the spell was broken. —Please, Catherine! I didn't mean for it to happen that way..I'm sorry—

My apology echoes off the trees and over to the cliffs that drop into the Pacific .. across the bay to where the city is waiting for us behind the fog .. traveling even beyond that but she still doesn't answer me.

When it's silent again, I listen.

Her footsteps have gone quiet and she's not running anymore.

I call her name again. I try apologizing over and over again. All of it is no use. She's hiding in the fog and I'll have to find her.

It feels like I have to find her or I'll stop breathing altogether .. like my life depends on being able to see her .. like watching the way she sleeps on her bed is what causes my heart to work .. the way she always has one arm bent under her head and the other dangling off the edge .. legs bent at the knees like white outlines on the sidewalk in a murder mystery.

The up and down of her chest as she breathes.

The little noises she makes in her sleep.

I keep the image in the front of my mind as I continue to say her name .. searching through the dark corners around every tree and rock. I try to imagine her and me as sunbeams .. bright yellow streaks across the sky .. like smiling colors holding hands and hoping we can still be that happy because I don't know if I can live without her near me.

≫ ≪

Sometimes the fog is so thick it's like all the lines and shapes in the world have disappeared. It comes so sudden sometimes, swallowing the city in a blink. I'd watch it approach from my bedroom window when I was younger. The way it moved was the way a monster would move sneaking out from under a bed or from a closet door left open just a tiny inch.

It terrified me, but I watched.

Henry taught me not to be afraid.

"I think the fog means people from Heaven want to visit us," he told me. I asked if he meant like ghosts but he shook his head. "Not really. More like all of Heaven coming down at once just to show us what it's like."

He promised to show me.

He taught me a game he called Hide-and-Seek in Heaven.

It was scary to play at first. I stood on the porch and watched him disappear in our yard. Then he'd call out for me to find him until I took small steps into the fog. I'd listen as he said, "Warmer. You're getting warmer," saying it more than necessary because he knew I needed his voice to keep me from running back into the house and hiding.

We haven't played that game in ten years, but we're playing it now.

I'm hiding.

"Warmer," I whisper silently to myself as Henry moves closer to the rocks I'm crouching behind. I'm worried he's getting too warm. That he's going to find me. Because the fog doesn't scare me like it used to. It's my protection. And this time Henry is the one who resembles something crawling out from under the bed.

I flinch every time he shouts from somewhere closer than before.

"Catherine!"

The echo sounds like an explosion tearing apart the cliffs behind me and sending them tumbling into the sea.

"Come out! I'm sorry!" he yells.

He doesn't sound sorry at all. He sounds angry like his eyes were when he kissed me. And for a second then, I saw what he saw. I know what he wants. He doesn't just want me here and now, he wants me forever. Even that won't ever be enough. He wants to swallow me the way I used to think the fog would. He wants to eliminate everything and everyone else that I care about so I will be his. Only his.

I can't be that for him.

I don't want to be that for him.

But it doesn't matter what I want, he's going to find me.

If I were playing the game by the rules, I would have to change "warm" to "hot" and say it aloud for him because he's close enough for me to make out the outline of his shadow hunting me.

He hears the twigs crack when I shuffle backward.

Then he hears my breathing and grabs me before I can run again.

"Let me go!" I holler but he holds me still.

"Hey. It's me," he says. "It's okay."

It's not him, though. It's not okay. His arms are crushing my ribs, squeezing the breath out and making me weak. He keeps asking me why I'm trying to get away, saying he's sorry but not showing it.

"You're hurting me," I say.

He says he'll let go if I promise to listen to him.

I nod and feel his arms slip away. I stay still but my eyes keep darting this way and that like a rabbit's, ready to run as he tells me he made a mistake. That he never should've let things go this far. That he should've told me how he felt from the beginning.

"Why didn't you?" I ask. My eyes still searching for a way to escape because I still don't trust the way his eyes are staring at me like they own me.

"I don't know," he says. "I was afraid."

He looks away. Stares up at the trees and then at the ground, waiting for me to say something but I don't know what to say. I don't know how he expects me to react. "Okay? So? What do you want me to do, Henry?"

"Can't we just go back to the way things were before? Forget about all this other stuff?" he says.

He tries to hold my hand then, but I refuse.

"No, we can't," I tell him. "I'm not ready to forget. I don't want to forget because everything that has happened has helped me grow. I won't throw that away no matter how awful some of it has been."

Henry gets quiet after that.

He shoves his hands deep into his pockets and faces the ground. His whole body takes the shape of an apology. It makes me feel terrible, like I'm breaking his heart, but I can't help it. I can't change the way I feel.

"You promised," he says. "We both promised to stay together forever."

"We're not six years old anymore," I tell him. "We've changed."

I knew it would upset him even before I said it, but it needed to be said. I need to get through to him even if it means hurting him.

He steps toward me. Close enough to make me feel his words

when he says, "You lied to me." A look in his eyes worse than any other I've ever seen. A meaner look than he's ever flashed at Hindley.

I back away.

My sneakers slip on the small stones near the edge of the cliff behind me. I beg him to stop. I tell him that the Henry I used to make promises to would never do this, would never come at me the way he is right now. Approaching me with nothing but hatred in his expression.

I take one more step before I start to lose my balance.

Plead with him once more before I start to fall but I can't get through to him and I feel my legs give out under me. And even though I don't fall very far, it still feels like flying. It feels like floating until my head hits the ground. Then there's a flash of white pain before I see anything again.

Everything else fades away then.

The pain is all that exists for a second until the world starts to come back into focus and I can see the fog beginning to lift over the bridge. The city is spread out in the distance. Buildings of all different sizes stretching into the sky and each of them twinkling like electric stars. They look near enough to touch when I reach out my hand and I wonder if this is what it's like to be one of the birds gliding above the bay.

Henry bends down and puts his arm under my head but I can't feel it.

I know I should be mad. I should push him away and yell at him but I don't feel that either. It's like my emotions have all burned out and everything seems suddenly peaceful. And I think maybe he was right all along. Maybe this is what he was trying to tell me. That if I let go, I'd see that things weren't as complicated as I made them out to be.

I try to tell Henry but it comes out all wrong.

It comes out only as words that don't go together like I want them to.

I can tell something's wrong by the way he's looking at me. By the way he stutters when he says my name, I can tell he's crying.

"Is something wrong?" I ask him.

When he doesn't answer, I know whatever it is, it must be bad.

"Am I okay?" I ask him because he's looking at me like I've broken in a million pieces. Nothing feels broken or bleeding. I don't feel anything at all actually.

He lifts me into his arms then. I can barely feel his touch, but it's enough for me to know it's really him. He's not the Henry who was shouting at me. Not anymore. He's the boy with midnight stars in his eyes again. He's the Henry that I dreamed of marrying so many times that I lost count.

"You're back," I say but he tells me not to speak.

"It's going to be all right," he says. He repeats it with each step as he carries me away. "I'm going to fix this."

I want to tell him that he already has but my mouth is too dry. There're no words left inside me. So I tell him with a smile instead. The smile that I've always saved only for him. Then I let my arms fall to my side like wings gliding just above the ground and I see him forcing a smile back at me. It's the last thing I see clearly before things start to go blurry. Everything but the stars. I can still see them even when I can't see anything else.

They get brighter as I move closer.

So bright that I have to close my eyes.

"I'm tired," I whisper.

Henry tells me I shouldn't go to sleep. But it's too hard to stay awake.

I have one last thing to tell him, though. Trying to get the strength together to find the words because I'm so tired suddenly but I need to say it now or I'll forget. I need to say it now when I still mean it.

"Henry? I'm ready to go with you now."

His hand is on the back of my head, gently pressing my face close to his heart so that I hear it beating. It sounds like singing. Like a song the ocean sings.

It's always been my favorite lullaby to fall asleep to.

EPILOGUE

The pages in the journal are blank from beginning to end even though I've had it for weeks. I'm supposed to write in it every day.. that's what the therapist says. He claims it will help me if I write about how I feel. But blank pages say it better than I ever could. That's how I feel.. like ghost words written on ghost paper.

—Don't think of it as a punishment— he says. —Think of it as a way of getting better— He's leaning forward.. his elbows draped on the desk between us.. the springs in the chair squealing like a dying balloon as he rocks.. wringing his hands together trying to stir up some enthusiasm in me.

I cough and lower my eyes to my lap.

Mr. Cheung fixes his glasses and sighs as he sits back in the chair again.. a look that says I've let him down again.

—We've been at this nearly nine months— he says.. getting up from the chair to reveal the black bold letters that tattoo everything in this place.. SAN FRANCISCO DEPARTMENT OF JUVENILE CORRECTIONS. It's branded onto the pens and onto my shirt.. on little signs above every door. I see it so often, it's branded onto the inside part of my eyelids. See them so clearly like a shadow over everything and I want to tear through it.. tear them apart and rearrange them to spell something different.. something meaningful that I can read once before the letters scatter.. blown away by nuclear wind and leave burn holes in the shadows.. something bright to seep through.. a window for me to stare through for the next 426 days.. stare so long that I go blind.

It seems like the perfect way to spend my time.

I've been sentenced to two years in here.. 730 days.. 304 have already gone. *Reckless endangerment*.. that's the term they used to sum up everything that happened the night Catherine died. I had to listen to witnesses telling the judge exactly what happened.. exactly how I was responsible even though none of them were there for her last breath.

The trial was all theater.. a set made to look real and actors playing parts.. saying their lines as the soundtrack flickered in and out behind them. No awards for any of them.. their characters too predictable.. not showing any range. Hindley stuck to the script. Red alcohol eyes blaring against the glare of the lights as he slurred his lies. Made up some story about me breaking in.. forcing Catherine against her will. A last-ditch chance to get back at me before he evaporated into a new life with a new family.

Isabelle played the victim in the role of a lifetime. Part she was made for.. the blue tint of her skin where I'd hit her..fluttering long eyelashes and the pretty pout of her mouth..showing all the signs of a terrified girl as the words quivered from her lips. It had nothing to do with me..all for the attention..for the sympathy. They listened with large ears..but they were tuned to the wrong frequency because they didn't hear Catherine.

I did.

Her six-year-old voice moving inside the walls..whispers telling everything about every yesterday she ever lived..telling me that none of this matters because she saw me differently..telling me to remember the last look in the last second of her eyes. —*We need each other*— she whispered but no one else heard it.

These are the kinds of thoughts Mr. Cheung thinks I should write down..scribble them on every inch of that little notebook so we can pore over them at these meetings. —Dissect them and piece them back together— he says..saying it will help piece me back together. They see me that way..like some kind of Humpty Dumpty shattered all over the ground..all the king's men and all their horses and the rest of it. Part of it's true but not the way they think..without Catherine, half of me is missing..that's not something they can fix with talking and taking notes.

Eventually time runs out the way it always does. Everything measured by the tick of the clock..scheduled and divided. It's just another way to keep me trapped and away from her. But time doesn't mean anything..time can't keep us apart.

On my way out, Mr. Cheung reminds me that he can't

help me if I don't want to help myself.. picking up the empty notebook from the table and handing it to me. —Just in case—

I put it in my pocket.

It will be blank again the next time we meet.. white like the halls in this building.. solid white tile from floor to ceiling. Bright sunlight and fluorescent lights to bleach everything in clean illumination. I like it.. wandering lost in the light it reminds me of walking through heavy fog on a summer morning. She's with me when I move through the halls.. the sour smell of her sheets fills the air.. the shape of her hand in mine when I drag my fingers along the wall.

—All right. In you go— the guard says. He holds the door open.. shuffling to the side to clear the way and I slip past him without a word.

The beds are lined up in two perfect rows from the door to the end of the room like benches in a bus station. I make my way to mine as the door clicks behind me. The outside world sealed off and I'm safe to wait for a ride to some other place. None of the other kids bother to look up from whatever they're doing. Most everyone just keeps to himself. Waiting same as me.

I never feel much like talking. Nelly's the only one who can get me to say more than a few words every so often on visiting days. I'll talk to her because she's the only one who understands. She's the only one who doesn't blame me. She knows how I feel about Catherine.. how I would never hurt her.

We never talk about Catherine, though.

We don't need to talk about it.

We both feel it without saying.

But those were long gone, yesterday's visiting days. She hasn't been in a while..not since..not after the last time when we both felt like ghosts passing along ghost words. Not saying anything..just talking..helping each other go separate ways because I don't belong in her world. It's probably better that she's vanished.

I fold my arms behind my head and lean back on my bunk.

The room buzzes with the sound of twenty other kids being alone. I drift within the noise..a comforting sound like rain falling on the roof of Catherine's bedroom once upon a time. I turn my head to the window and let my eyes adjust to the sunlight..let my gaze travel from the top of one building to the next until everything goes slightly out of focus.

A glimpse of the Golden Gate Bridge pokes above the horizon. It's easier to see at night when it's all lit up..but I see her better during the day..Catherine gliding between the steel beams like a shooting star. And I watch her for hours like I used to watch her from outside her room when she thought she was alone..her door open a crack..just enough for me to see her sitting in front of the mirror and I'd watch the way her hair slid through her fingers as she pouted and pretended to kiss her reflection..the way her eyes fluttered as she mouthed secret words to imaginary people.

She always knew I was watching her.

She knows it now too.

She's waiting for me..her ghost staying on the bridge where she died, waiting for me to join her the way we always promised. Whispering to me in words that even satellites can't hear.. tiny words that travel only from her into me.. telling me that we have to keep our promises because maybe we were only meant to be together after we are part of the sky. Maybe love is something that we can't have until we die.

—*Dreams become more real the more you dream them*— she tells me when I close my eyes.. her voice louder than anything else I can hear.

I'm getting closer to her every day.

Closer now than ever before and then we'll be alone together. Because she needs me like I need her. We need each other if we're ever going to be like the birds soaring above the waves.. above all the shit that kept us apart and never looking back as we climb higher.

It's a promise we made so many times that it can't be broken.

It's a promise I'm making again each time I look for her off in the distance.. one she makes back by making herself visible.. making me smile.. smiling as I roll onto my side.. smiling for the future.

One day we'll be together and everything will be the way it was always meant to be. One day the two of us will be like stars shooting across the sky.. holding hands on our way into Heaven.

Discussion Questions

1. The author has a unique way of writing dialogue, not calling attention to it with quote marks, the way most authors do. How does this work as a device in the writing? What does this subtlety say about Henry and his interaction with others?

2. Henry and Hindley have an immediate rivalry when Henry is taken in by the Earnshaws. Why is Catherine able to adapt to Henry so quickly, but Hindley is not? Why does this rivalry intensify over the years instead of fading? Catherine is unable to side with either her brother or Henry. Does she blame them equally for their rivalry?

3. How does the first chapter of Catherine's narration, where she talks about the freedom of the birds right before being told of her father's death, foreshadow Catherine's own fate at the end of the story?

4. At one point in the story, Henry says of Catherine, "She'll belong only to me and I won't have to share her anymore." Is this ultimately the reason Henry loses Catherine?

5. What does the symbolism of the fish and the birds—in which Henry is the fish and Catherine is the birds—mean for Henry and Catherine's relationship during the course of the book, and afterward? Why do the fish represent Henry?

6. By the end of the story, when Henry is a "slave" to Hindley, Catherine is sad, but scarcely sticks up for him. How has Hindley corrupted her mind so that she believes Henry could be turning into a bad person? Has Henry's behavior reaffirmed this idea? And how is this the critical mistake Catherine makes?

7. Catherine's tragic death is an example of what loving someone too much can do. How do Henry and Catherine's actions lead up to this point? Are they both responsible?

Discussion of *The Heights,*
as it compares to *Wuthering Heights*

1. In both *The Heights* and *Wuthering Heights,* how do Henry and Catherine/Heathcliff and Cathy express that they are destined to be together? Compare the sense of fate that surrounds the characters in both books.

2. In *Wuthering Heights,* Emily Brontë creates a reverse heaven and hell, in which the moor and Cathy's home at Wuthering Heights are heaven (but described as a hellish place), and the beautiful and refined Thrushcross Grange is hell (which would seem like heaven to most people). How has Brian James taken a similar idea and used it to define Henry and Catherine's relationship?

3. Why does Brian James describe Catherine as a bird? What are the characteristics of a bird that contribute to Catherine's personality—and her ultimate fate? How does Emily Brontë use symbolism to represent Cathy or Heathcliff?

4. Cathy in *Wuthering Heights* is mischievous, tomboyish, and, at times, hard and cold—the direct opposite of how Henry portrays Catherine in *The Heights.* Why does Brian James chose to soften Catherine's edges? Or is this the perspective Heathcliff has always had of Cathy?

5. Brian James set his story in San Francisco. What is it about this city that relates to Emily Brontë's moors? Would it be possible to tell a modern story in the original location?

6. In *Wuthering Heights,* the story continues with the second generation—Heathcliff uses Cathy's daughter to achieve his ultimate revenge. If Brian James continued with the second generation of this family, where would the story would go?

SQUARE FISH

For more information about Square Fish books, authors, and illustrators visit
www.squarefishbooks.com.

GOFISH

BRIAN JAMES

What did you want to be when you grew up?

Like most kids my age, I wanted to be a Jedi Knight, or a space smuggler with my own spaceship and a furry alien as a best friend. Alas, technology didn't avance as rapidly as my imagination anticipated.

When did you realize you wanted to be a writer?

I was around eleven years old when I started wanting to be a writer. It was sort of an odd desire considering that, at the time, I didn't really like to read all that much. But I loved coming up with stories that I used to create while playing with action figures. I'd set up these elaborate plots that would take days and days for me to play out. Around that age is when I began to have the urge to write these stories down.

What's your most embarrassing childhood memory?

When I was in fifth grade, my best friend tape-recorded a phone conversation where I admitted to liking a certain girl. Of course, I knew he was recording it. It was actually a plan that we came up with together. The second part of the plan was getting him to play it for everyone at recess. It seemed easier to admit that I liked her if I could pretend I was being betrayed. However, that didn't make it any less embarrassing when the whole fifth grade heard it the next day. The girl handled it with class, which only made me like her more.

As a young person, who did you look up to most?
My mother. She did everything.

What was your worst subject in school?
I was lucky enough not to have any "bad" subjects. I always did well in school. But, ironically, my worst subject was definitely Spelling. I'm still a horrible speller, so I'm very thankful for spell check.

What was your best subject in school?
Probably math and science, though I never really enjoyed either of them. But for some reason, they both came easily to me. English classes took much more effort on my part, which is most likely why they kept my interest.

What was your first job?
Babysitting. I have two younger brothers and two younger sisters. So I was a de facto babysitter very often. But my first real job was as a lifeguard when I was a teenager. I also taught swimming lessons to toddlers; the patience required for that job certainly helped prepare me to be a writer.

How did you celebrate publishing your first book?
Honestly, I'm still celebrating. Every time I look at any of my books, I'm very thankful.

Where do you write your books?

I have an office in my house where I do all of my work. The room is filled with books, music, and toys. All the walls are covered with photos, pictures from magazines, drawings I've done, and letters from kids . . . it's sort of like an external portrait of what goes on in my head.

Where do you find inspiration for your writing?

Anywhere and everywhere. I get inspiration from other art, be it music, literature, film, or visual art. I also find inspiration in the world around me. Any little thing can be inspiring if you take the time to look at it. I like to keep a notebook on me at all times and write down ideas because I never know when a passing stranger or a bit of conversation will spark my imagination.

Which of your characters is most like you?

In varying degrees, all of my characters are somewhat based on me, or aspects of my personality. However, Brendon from *Pure Sunshine* is very much me. It's the most autobiographical book I've written.

When you finish a book, who reads it first?

My wife is always the first person to read anything I write. After she reads it, I usually do another draft before anyone else ever sees it.

Are you a morning person or a night owl?

Certainly NOT a morning person . . . in my younger days, I'd say I was a night owl. Though now, I'm solidly a day person.

What's your idea of the best meal ever?

A twenty-course dinner with every kind of food . . . so much food that I'd explode if I ate it all. There'd have to be Asian food,

Hispanic food, seafood, gourmet dishes, and good old American cuisine like pizza, burgers, and fries. Then I'd wash it all down with a sundae of chocolate chip ice cream, hot fudge, peanut butter topping, whipped cream and one of those fake cherries on top.

Which do you like better: cats or dogs?
Growing up, I was always a dog person. I had two dogs as a child. Now I have two cats. I could never choose between the two. They're both so different and both have so much to offer.

What do you value most in your friends?
Intellect and open-mindedness.

Where do you go for peace and quiet?
I live in a remote part of the Catskills, so there's no lack of peace and quiet. If I'm feeling even more in need of seclusion, a long hike through the mountains is as good as it gets.

What makes you laugh out loud?
Junie B. Jones, Homer Simpson, and *It's Always Sunny in Philadelphia*.

What's your favorite song?
I'm a music junkie and have a collection of a few thousand CDs, so choosing a favorite song might be the hardest task for me to imagine. I couldn't even tell you my favorite album without naming at least twenty or so.

Who is your favorite fictional character?
Addie Pray from *Paper Moon*.

What are you most afraid of?
Any evil that cloaks itself in an elaborate disguise.

What time of year do you like best?
Winter. I love cold, grey, snowy weather and always have. I've read that people most enjoy the season they were born in . . . at least for me, that theory holds true.

What's your favorite TV show?
I think *Lost* is the most creative show on the air. So many television shows assume viewers are dumb. It's one of the few shows that assumes its viewers are smart and can handle big ideas. I'm also a nut for *Doctor Who* and *Battlestar Galactica*.

If you were stranded on a desert island, who would you want for company?
My wife. We've never run out of things to say and she's the only person I've ever met whose company I never grow tired of at any point.

If you could travel in time, where would you go?
The future . . . WAY in the future . . . as far as it would take for long-distance space travel to be possible.

What's the best advice you have ever received about writing?
Strangely enough, it wasn't meant to be advice. A teacher (not one of mine) tried to discourage me from pursing writing because he said there were only about a thousand people that could make a living as a writer and asked if I really thought I was one of them. I thought about it for a second and decided that, yes, I did think I was one of them. And whenever I've felt discouraged, I remember that conversation and it always helps

me regain my confidence. I think in order to achieve anything, you need first believe that you can.

What do you want readers to remember about your books?

Whatever is important to them. I think that's the great thing about art. It's a fulfillment of personal creativity that people respond to their own personal way. For me, what readers take away from my books isn't too important. As long as the book is meaningful to them in some way, that's all that matters to me. That the book has some personal meaning for them is the greatest compliment a writer can get.

What would you do if you ever stopped writing?

Probably teach, though I'm not sure I'd like it . . . so I'm going to hope it never comes to that.

What do you like best about yourself?

The fact that I've never completely lost the ability to be a child.

What is your worst habit?

Smoking. It's such a disgusting habit that I've been able to scale back but never quite kick. My biggest regret in life is that I ever started.

What is your best habit?

I'm a clean person without being a freak about it.

What do you consider to be your greatest accomplishment?

I like to think I haven't reached my greatest accomplishment yet. I still believe that the best work I've done is always the latest. By

never feeling that I've accomplished anything, it keeps me moti-
vated to keep striving.

Where in the world do you feel most at home?
New York City. I lived there for ten years before I moved away for
a variety of reasons. But anytime I'm ever there, I feel that I belong.

What do you wish you could do better?
Sing. I'd give anything to be able to sing.

**What would your readers be most surprised to learn
about you?**
I'm not-so-distantly related to Jesse James.

If Hannah doesn't watch her back, she's going to be blonde and popular and dead— just like all the other zombies in this town.

THEY'RE BEAUTIFUL. THEY'RE POPULAR. THEY'RE DEAD.

Keep reading for an excerpt from

ZOMBIE BLONDES
by BRIAN JAMES

available now in paperback from Square Fish.

ONE

I can usually pick out the popular kids soon after setting foot into a new school. The girls, anyway. They wear popularity like a uniform for everyone to see. From their hairstyles to their expensive shoes. Everything about them is torn from the glossy pages of the latest teen fashion magazines. Everything about them is perfect. At least on the outside, anyway.

The boys are a little trickier.

Their looks have only a small part to play in deciding their place in the social order of things. What they're into is just as important as how they look. Depends on what kind of school it is, too. There are as many different kinds of high schools as there are different kinds of cliques in each one. There's the artsy sort of schools where the skinny, mysterious boys are the ones who get all the attention. Then there's the college-prep kind of schools where class rank and GPA go hand in hand with a boy's cute looks to determine where he stands with the girls. At thug schools and drug schools, the more damaged or dangerous a boy is makes all the difference. Last, but not least, there're jock schools like Maplecrest where all that really counts is how good a guy is at sports. Even if he's zit faced and moronic, a boy can be popular here, so it could take some time to figure it all out.

But with girls it doesn't matter so much what kind of school it is. It's always the thinnest, prettiest ones wearing the least amount of clothing that the dress code allows who rule the hallways. Because boys' tastes don't change much just because they like painting more than sports. So it's always the girls pretty enough to put on a postcard that get to be one of the Perfect People. The social elite. The clique that runs the school. The ones who get away with everything by batting their eyelashes and pretending not to know any better. They get to decide which of the other girls are okay to talk to and which should be teased into having an eating disorder.

Different schools but always the same thing.

Those are the girls I need to impress if I want to be popular, or keep from pissing off if I just wish to fit in. That makes figuring out who they are pretty important. Highest priority if I wish to avoid making a mistake that will get me on the wrong list unintentionally. A dirty look is all it takes. It's the way it's been at every school I've passed through in the last couple of years, so I've gotten pretty good at figuring out who they are. My social well-being depends on it.

Maplecrest might be the easiest school yet.

I know who the most popular girl is the second I see her.

One look is all it takes. Her long blond curls like a halo when the sunlight shines on her just right. Perfect smile and perfect skin like an angel made of porcelain. Sparkling blue eyes with soft pink eyelids to match the strawberry pout of her upper lip. The slender curve of her shoulder and fragile shape of her knees peeking out from the bottom of her short skirt. She's delicate like a bird as she glides through the cafeteria. Every pair of eyes following her as she soars to the table crowded with other pretty girls who just look like lesser clones once she joins them.

I don't need to know her name or anything about her to know she's the It Girl in school. It's written all over the faces of her friends as they wait their turn for her to say hi to them. Each and every one trying so hard to look exactly like she does. Each of them pretty, too. Each of them wearing the same bleached hair and bleached skin but with a little less twinkling in their eyes, making them a little less perfect.

And even though I promised myself I wouldn't do it this time, I start comparing myself with them, the Perfect People. I can't help it. I have to know where I stand. Crummy town or not, I care what people think of me. It's a bad habit. My dad calls it teenage-girl sickness and says there's a cure for it. I tell him I know there is, but that I don't really want to end up being a crazy cat lady when I get older.

I twist my hair around my finger and stare at the split ends. Mine doesn't have the same shine and it's not nearly as blond. Mine's more like dirty straw than a golden halo. And my eyes are muddy, too, and look nothing like the sky the way the popular-table girls' do. All of them so blond and beautiful, like little figurines too precious to let children play with.

I push my tray away. I'm not hungry anymore.

It's not that I think I'm ugly or anything. I know I'm cute enough. And I don't want to be the prettiest girl in school or anything like that. It's just that I don't even come close. Not to their leader or even to her tagalongs. I thought in a small, time-forgotten town like this that I'd at least have a shot. It's not really that important to me, it's just that it's easier being new in a school if you're one of the prettiest girls. I hoped maybe this time I'd get lucky. But that dream vanished the instant I saw her.

"Her name's Maggie Turner," a voice says in my ear as if reading my thoughts. Not startling me enough to scream, but just enough to squeak like a little mouse.

I turn my head to see a scrawny-looking boy with shaggy straw hair dressed in shabby clothes. I recognize him from one of my classes. Takes me a second to place him. Geometry, third period. The kid a few rows over who kept looking at me so much that I just stopped checking after a while. He's not so bad looking, but he's not exactly my type, either. Long and lanky and a little on the creepy side. And before I can make up my mind whether I want to tell him to get lost or not, he pulls up the empty chair and sits down next to me.

"Maggie Turner," he says again. "You're wondering what her name is, aren't you?" I'm not sure what to say. I wasn't really expecting company. First day in a new school mostly equals isolation, especially in the lunchroom. It's one of the symptoms of the new-kid disease. Everybody wants to talk about you, but nobody wants to talk to you. Not at first anyway and his surprise visit catches me off guard. Not to mention the fact that he knew what I was thinking about.

"I was just . . . ," I start to say but never finish.

"You were just staring at Maggie Turner like everyone else," he says and I can feel my face turning red.

It's not that I mind getting caught or that I'm embarrassed about being fascinated with the popular girls. I just don't know if I want to share it with some skinny, weird kid who wanders the lunchroom searching for girls he doesn't know to sit next to. But whatever the reason, my cheeks start to blush and he begins to notice.

"It's okay," he says. "She's an attention magnet. Everyone likes to stare at her." He puts his hands behind his head and leans back. Tilts the chair until it's resting against the wall and settles in like we're long-lost pals.

"Look, what do you want?" I ask in a snotty tone because at this point all I really want is for him to go away. I'd rather be lonely than sit with him. He sort of gives me the creeps. I even slide my chair a few inches away. Too bad he can't take a hint, though. He's either a little dense or else he has the beginnings of a crush on me. With my luck, it wouldn't surprise me. I'm never a magnet for attention so much as I'm a magnet for weirdos.

He puts his hands back on the table and lets the chair ease back down to the floor. Then he hunches over and leans closer to me like he's going to tell me a secret or something.

"Today's your first day, right?" he asks.

I'm not sure what that has to do with anything but I nod my head anyway.

"Well, I'm just trying to help you out, that's all," he says.

"Help me how?" I ask. I don't see him helping me out at all. The only thing he's doing is keeping any normal people from talking to me.

"I can tell you want to be friends with her," he says. I feel like arguing that I don't even know her and that he doesn't even know me, so how can he make that assumption. But deep down I know he's kind of right, so I don't bother. Besides, he knows he's right the same way I knew about Maggie being the It Girl in the first place. He can spot people like me just like I can spot the popular.

"So what if I do?" I ask him. "Is that a crime or something?"

"No," he says. "I just thought I'd try to save you from Maggie Turner's clutches before it's too late."

I can't help but smile a little, because I've seen this trick before. Get close to the new girl and scare her with tales of the evil clique. It's always the outsiders like him that try it. The malcontents. But that's all it is. A trick. Try to claim me for their own and poison me to the rest of the school. Still, though, he is sort of cute and he is the only person to talk to me all day, so I decide to humor him, anyway.

"Yeah, why's that?" I ask.

"Because Maggie isn't like the rest of us," he says in a whisper. Really getting into the part and looking around as if he's checking to make sure no one is listening. "She's not like real people, she's better. She was born on Christmas. Her favorite color is pink. Baby pink, not porno pink. And it doesn't matter how cold it is outside, she always wears short skirts and short tops and no one has ever once seen her shiver. She never eats anything but carrots, at least not in public. And though she doesn't have any proven super-powers, all her friends follow her like they're in some kind of cult. Plus, she just happens to be the captain of the cheer-leading squad and is one evil bitch on top of that."

I fold my arms across the table and rest my head. Open my eyes wide and give him all my attention like a little kid at story time. "You seem to know a lot about her for not liking her," I say with a little smile but I think the sarcasm escapes him.

"Everyone does, she makes sure of it," he says. No longer whispering and no longer playful like before. A little angry even as he taps the edge of the table with his knuckles.

"Let me guess," I say because it's my turn to play a little game with him. "Every boy has the hots for her, includ-ing you."

"Not me," he says without hesitating. Says it like a fact, never taking his eyes off her. Says it the way I can tell it's not just a denial. Says it so I know he doesn't just not like her, he despises her.

"But you did at one point," I say because I can tell that, too. "And she didn't like you, so now you hate her." No-body gives the kind of look he does to someone like Mag-gie Turner unless they're jealous or scorned. I can't see him being the kind of boy jealous of popularity, but he certainly looks like the emotional type who gets his feelings hurt.

I may have hurt them some, too, because he pushes his chair away from the table and half stands up. He's about to walk away but stops. Turns to me and opens his mouth and starts to stutter like he's not sure if he should say what he wants to. Then finally deciding to go ahead and say it, but refusing to take his eyes off the floor when he does. "It's just . . . you're kind of pretty . . . and she might try to turn you into one of them . . . one of her clones," he says. "I don't want to see that happen to you, that's all."

I tuck my lip under my top teeth.

"Is that supposed to be a compliment?" I ask.

"Nope," he says. "Just a warning."

I stare at him in silence and he stares back. Stares into my eyes for the first time since coming over to me. Something blank in his expression that doesn't make sense to me. He's either the most socially challenged boy I've ever met, or one of the cleverest. Whichever it is, he's by far the most interesting thing about this town so far.

He takes a step away before stopping. Makes a gesture like he forgot something and comes back. "My name's Lukas, by the way," he says.

"You know, you're really supposed to do that before you start pestering strange girls," I say.

"Yeah? Well, this is Maplecrest," he says.

"What does that have to do with anything?" I ask.

"You'll see," he says. "A lot of things in Maplecrest are done differently."

He starts to drift away again and this time I stop him. "Don't you want to know my name?" I ask him.

"It's Hannah," he says. Then he smiles for the first time. And I'm a little surprised, but he actually has kind of a sweet smile. "I was paying attention in class when the teacher called your name," he explains.

"Oh. Right," I say, remembering third period for the second time. "Well, thanks for the warning," I say with just enough attitude for him to know I'm not being completely serious.

"Do yourself a favor and stay away from them," he says with just enough attitude to let me know he's being deadly serious. Then he disappears into the crowd of faces, leaving me alone to listen to the million fragments of conversations happening all around me until the bell rings.